Trapped in an 80s Teen Movie

by Michelle Duffy

Dedicated to my husband Karl, whose unstinting support and exhortations to leave the housework alone have made this book possible.

1

Julie's life had not turned out as glamorous as she thought it would be.

Dust blew in the open door of Chili Go-Go's, the behemoth outlet store that sold one thousand varieties of hot sauce. The breeze coming through was hotter than anything on the shelves but Dirk, the creepy manager, had decided that an open door was more welcoming than functioning aircon.

And cheaper.

Julie leaned over the counter and licked a bead of sweat from her top lip. Across her chest was emblazoned the legend, *Get Some Hot Stuff*.

She watched the store's lone customer stumble through the aisles towards her. Short dreads, moon tan, unfocused eyes—this guy was operating on an herbal frequency.

He fell into the counter, till Julie thought he would just about kiss the glass; then miraculously he straightened himself up, all jangled limbs, a trail of cartoon drool still connecting him to the surface.

"Can I help you?"

The stoner looked up, surprised to see her. His eyes gradually swam into focus, one at a time.

"Yeah... Umm..."

Professional face, thought Julie, professional face. But really, why bother? Who was watching her anyway?

Then she remembered – Dirk's new CCTV cameras, which he'd had installed as both security devices and 'staff training aids'. She'd bet her measly paycheck he'd installed a hidden one in the staff bathroom.

"Did you want to buy some hot sauce?"

A tiny little LED lightbulb flashed behind the stoner's eyes. "Yeah! Yeah, hot sauce, alright! What's.....?"

As he trailed off again, Julie bit back a cry of frustration. She followed his eyes as they wandered around the store, searching for his lost thought. Suddenly they snapped back to Julie's face, along with a big goofy grin.

"What's, like, your hottest hot sauce?"

With the relief of finally having something she could deal with, Julie reached under the counter for a bottle and slipped easily into her long-memorized store spiel:

"Shaky Sheedy's Sheer Death by Chili measures sixteen million units on the Scoville scale. It will blister your skin on contact. If you wish to purchase this highly collectible item, you must sign a waiver stating that you understand that it must only be used as an ingredient and will never be consumed neat."

And breathe.

As Julie placed the bottle with its skull-shaped stopper on the counter, the stoner reached for it. "So, can I try it on a chip?"

Julie fought back a gag as his long, filthy fingernails scratched and rummaged through the complimentary basket of tortilla chips on the countertop. Not that she would ever eat them, but she'd seen other people try them, nice people. People who wash.

"No. I would not advise that you try it on a chip. There would be a high risk of severe injury and possibly death."

"So, umm... I can't try it on a chip?"

What could you say to that? Luckily, Julie didn't have to say anything, she was saved by the bell - the phone began to holler from the office behind the counter.

"Excuse me, I have to get that." Turning to go, a thought struck her. She turned back and grabbed the bottle of Sheer Death, hiding it back behind the glass. She pointed one finger at the stoner. "Do not touch that."

Julie forced a smile as she picked up the phone – another of Dirk's rules. "Hi, Chili Go-Go's, world's hottest hot sauces. How may I help you today?"

"Julie, that you?"

Julie stifled a sigh. It was her husband, Roger. And she'd bet he didn't just call to say he loved her. She twisted a loose section of hair around her first two fingers - same way she always did when she knew she was in for trouble - and tested the waters. "Hi Honey, everything okay?"

"Julie, did you remember to buy my corn muffins?"

"Oh shit, no, I'm sorry, Honey. I forgot."

"Well could you pick some up on the way home?"

Really? He was calling her at work just to get her to run to the store for him and get corn muffins?

"Oh Roger, you know I'm at Rosanna's tonight."

There was an ominous pause. "Since when?"

"Well, since every Friday, since always. Friday night is movie night, y'know?" Glancing up, Julie saw the stoner kid creeping around the counter and reaching for the skull-stoppered bottle. "Hey you, knock it off!"

"What?"

"Oh not you, Roger. Look, I have to go, there's this…"

Roger cut her off. "I just don't understand how you could forget those corn muffins. You were at the store yesterday. How hard is it? It's because it was only important to me, isn't it, you didn't even remember…"

Julie was trying to pay attention, she really was, but the stoner kid had got ahold of the *three hundred dollar* bottle of hot sauce and was tossing it up, catching it one-handed behind his back.

Torn between not wanting to make the row worse, and not wanting to have to pay for a broken collector's item, she heard Roger shouting from the phone, "Well? Well??"

"I'm sorry, Honey…"

"Well, what am I going to do now?"

"You, ah… You could go to the store?"

What Roger said to his dear sweet wife probably isn't worth repeating, but she didn't hear it anyway.

Seeing the stoner upend a *lot* of Sheer Death sauce onto a chip, she dropped the phone and rushed to stop him from putting the damn thing in his mouth.

She was too late.

The second the sauce hit his tongue, that dumbass kid dropped to the floor screaming like the devil's fork was in his very gonads.

So Julie did the only thing she could do: she grabbed the soda siphon from behind the counter and started squirting straight into his mouth.

* * *

Across town, Rosanna looked out across the roomful of high school seniors, slumped at various levels of boredom.

It was always like this at the start of the year; they'd all adopt a pose of complete indifference, a protective posture to avoid ever risking having an opinion and getting it wrong.

Geez, thought Rosanna, when did kids all get so afraid of what people thought of them? Aren't they supposed to be fearless, impassioned, telling me how my generation got it all wrong and how they're gonna show me the truth about life?

Or maybe that was just a movie she'd seen.

Still, every year there'd be one or two students who made it worth it. Who gradually came out of their shells and – with a lot of encouragement – would start to express ideas. Sometimes even their own ideas.

With this in mind, she turned back to the picture projected onto the wall behind her: Picasso's *Demoiselles D'Avignon*. "It's hard for us to see this painting with fresh eyes now, but at the time Picasso's style was so different, so shocking, it changed the visual world forever. But why did Picasso paint this way?"

A skinny little Heavy Metal headbanger, Garrison, half raised his hand.

Garrison? thought Rosanna, really? He wasn't normally a big contributor. But hey… "Yes, Garrison?"

"Well, uh…" Garrison smirked, "uh, he couldn't paint properly?"

The little weasel snickered, and the rest of the class started to join in. Rosanna opened her mouth to respond, but the bell rang out for the end of class.

Like a miracle, the class full of Lazarus' rose from the dead, ramming pads, pencils, books into their bags.

"Hey!" Rosanna raised her hand, trying to stem the tide of the undead. "Hey, did I say you guys could pack up? We're not finished yet."

Rosanna threw up her hands in frustration. She might as well have said nothing at all. Raising her voice against the scrape of chairs, she called out, "Okay, everybody, remember to leave your portfolios on my desk for grading as you leave."

Then she gave up, sat behind the desk and picked up a book as the students streamed past, dumping heavy portfolios as they went.

Already mentally in the Monday classes, planning the 11th-grade sculpture session, Rosanna was startled by a small cough.

Looking up, she saw Roy, a skater kid with an intelligent face. She had a good feeling about Roy; he was going to be one of the good ones this year, she just knew it. He'd loitered at the end of the line and was fidgeting for her attention as he put his heavy folder on the desk.

"Miss Peterson?"

"Yes, Roy?" Rosanna stood and started to gather the portfolios. Roy was a nice kid but still, it was Friday afternoon and she was nearly as keen to get out of there as the students.

"Well, er, I just wanted to say that I like your class. You're pretty much the best teacher here."

Rosanna felt her cheeks pink up with pleasure and a smile started to creep across her face. "Well, thank you, Roy."

Roy shuffled, embarrassed. "Yeah, some of the other teachers here, they just teach like they're reading out of a textbook.... Well, they're pretty shit."

She felt the smile freeze on her face.

"So, yeah, I guess what I'm saying is, you're definitely the least shit teacher here."

Rosanna's cheeks ached as her frozen smile curdled into one of wry acceptance. "Huh. Well, it's not 'Oh Captain, My Captain', Roy, but it'll have to do."

Roy stared at her, the reference flying right over his head, but Rosanna had had enough for one day. She scooped all of the portfolios into her arms and headed for the door.

* * *

Julie raised her hand over her eyes, squinting into the evening sun as paramedics chairlifted the stoner kid into the waiting ambulance. The entire soda siphon and a whole block of cream cheese hadn't been enough to stop the chemical warfare that Shaky Sheedy's Sheer Death had unleashed on that poor, stupid kid's throat.

She jumped a little as a warm hand rested on her shoulder and turned to see Red, her co-slave at the store, named for her untamed mane of flaming (dyed) red hair. Julie should have known; Red was kind, but she was loud and her perfume was louder. How had she not smelled her coming?

Red patted her, trying to offer some comfort. "Hey Jules, look at it this way: in a hundred years' time, who's gonna care?"

Julie smiled wryly, still staring into the sun. "Me, cause I'll have been unemployed for a hundred years."

She turned to the older woman, handing her a giant bunch of keys. "Would you be a doll and lock up? I gotta go."

Climbing into her car – with a giant chili pepper on the roof and '1000 Varieties of Hot Sauce' emblazoned across the doors, it wouldn't be hers for much longer – Julie finally had a little time to reflect on her row with Roger.

God, if only she could just articulate what she wanted to say to him, when she wanted to say it, but she'd never been good at fights. She just got so upset that she couldn't think straight, and by the time she did think what she wanted to say, it seemed a little childish to be bringing it up again, so long after the fact.

But it really stuck in her craw, Roger saying she didn't remember the things that were important to him. Important to him? she wanted to scream right now. Important to him? What about him remembering the things that were important to her, like her birthday? Or what flowers she liked?

Or the fact that she was thirty-nine years old and all her eggs were just about to go pop, pop, pop because he seemed to have forgotten that when they'd gotten married – TEN YEARS AGO – they had also agreed to have children?

Right now, though, she was already late for Rosanna's and she knew that by the time she saw him tomorrow, it'd be too late to be starting this argument again.

But next time, definitely. She was going to tackle this once and for all. And she wasn't going to be put off by any excuses this time. She just had to wait for when the time was right and then she would bring it up.

Definitely.

She barely even noticed the ocean road going past as she took the familiar route to Rosanna's house. All these years after high school and they were still stuck in Delaware.

Sure, it was nice, they lived near the beach, crime was almost non-existent (except for drunk driving, but no one ever got arrested for that since they put all the cops on mountain bikes) and there was plenty of tax-free shopping.

But it wasn't exactly what she and Rosanna had planned when they were seventeen...

2

Rosanna grinned as she saw the Chili-mobile pull up in front of her house.

She ducked under the breakfast bench and hauled out her enormous blender. On a hot, sweaty day like today, only an ice-cold frozen smoothie was going to hit the spot. Feeling virtuous, Rosanna pulled a salad tray full of fruit out of the fridge and began to chop.

"Hey Rosanna!" Julie pushed through the kitchen door, bearing an enormous cake.

Rosanna's health kick halo wavered as she looked at the light glinting off the white, creamy frosting. Julie was just the best at baking. Should have been at home with a dozen rugrats round her feet, demanding more of mama's cookies; she would have loved that.

Rosanna sighed inwardly as she thought of Julie's husband, Roger, in low-slung pants and a skater top like he was still a teenager and not a paunchy forty-two year old Customer Service manager at the Outlet Stores management company. Someone should tell him that his baseball caps might hide the bald spot, but they didn't reverse time.

But who was she to criticize anyone's choice of husband? Hers was long gone – Jake had walked out when their son, Gib, was five but mentally and emotionally he'd been out the door the minute she said she was pregnant.

Yeah, he did the 'right thing', married her and all, but it hadn't exactly been the romance of the century.

Having a wife and kid was apparently cramping his rockstar ambitions.

Last she'd heard, Jake said he was 'working in IT', which was a euphemism for unemployed if the sketchy maintenance checks were anything to go by.

Still, it wasn't all bad, she thought as Gib himself came barging through the back door. Fifteen now and turning into a real heartbreaker, if he'd just wipe that surly look off of his face.

Julie smiled at her favorite (well, only) godson. "Hey, Gib."

Gib didn't even look up, just kept on moving through. "Don't bother," Rosanna apologized. "Unless there's a touch screen on your forehead, he can't see you."

Looking up from dumping a ton of fruit and ice in the blender, she saw a dubious look on Julie's face. "Don't worry," she reassured her, "this is going to be the most amazing frozen smoothie you have ever had. I'm gonna drop some linseed in here, some blue-green algae. It's gonna rock your digestive system."

Strangely, Julie's face remained doubtful. "Does that mean I'll poop a lot?" She put the cake down on the breakfast bar and peered into the blender.

"That's a lot of cake."

Julie's face turned from doubt to mischief in a moment. "Well, if you're on a health kick, you don't have to have any. But it's a real moist carrot cake; the middle layer is cream cheese frosting and a layer of Bender's Butt-Burnin' Hot Sauce."

Now it was Rosanna's turn to look skeptical. "Hot sauce?"

"Trust me." Julie scooped some creamy frosting on her finger and licked it right off.

"Well," said Rosanna, "you are the Queen of hot sauce and I bow to your higher judgment." Mocking her friend, she gave her a little flourishing bow, but Julie wasn't put off.

"Yup, lucky me. I can name one thousand varieties of hot sauce in Scoville ranking order."

"Well, beat that."

Watching Julie taking out plates and forks for the cake, as comfortable here as in her own home, something was niggling at the back of Rosanna's mind. Something she had to tell Julie? Give Julie? Suddenly, she remembered and reached for her purse.

"I've got that twenty I owe you."

"Twenty?" Julie poked her head up over the kitchen counter.

"Yeah, for the tickets, the thing, the gallery last week?"

Unconcerned, Julie went back to rummaging in the cupboard. "Shit Rosanna, call it an early birthday present. Hmm?"

Not getting an answer, Julie peeked up again. Rosanna was frozen over the purse. "Hey Ro, what's up?"

"I had fifty dollars in here. I can't find it." Rosanna felt a hot anger start to thaw the icy shock she'd gotten when she realized her money was gone – *again*. She tipped the bag upside down and shook the contents all over the counter, not caring as they spilled to the floor.

"I don't believe this." But she did believe it – it wasn't the biggest surprise. She slammed the bag down on the counter.

"GIIIIIBBB! Gibson Patrick Lane, you get down here right now!"

Julie winced as she heard a crash from upstairs and seconds later Gib slouched into the kitchen, a picture of whatever in his *Dew-Me Beach* t-shirt.

"What?" Gib's scowl didn't suggest either guilt or contrition.

Rosanna got straight to the point. "Where's my money?"

"What money? God!"

"The fifty bucks that was in my purse. Hand it over."

"You don't even know that was me. Why don't you ask Aunt Julie if she took it?"

Julie gave him a look that would freeze lava, but it didn't even give Gib pause.

"Whatever, you're not my real aunt." As he turned back to his mom, Julie resisted the childish urge to flip him the bird behind his back. How did Rosanna put up with this shit? She saw her friend's hand shaking as she gripped the counter, struggling for control.

"Gib, why do you need do this? I give you everything you want." She paused, not sure she wanted an answer to the next question. "Is it drugs?"

Gib rolled his eyes in total contempt. "Mom, you just don't get it."

"Get it? Get what?"

But Rosanna was already talking to an empty space, a swinging door where her son had been. She rounded on Julie. "God, is it me? I have tried so hard to be a friend to that boy and I end up sounding just like my mom – nag, nag, nag. Jesus!"

Gib has enough friends, thought Julie, but there are

some things you just don't say out loud, not even to your best friend. What could she say?

Rosanna ducked under the breakfast bench and Julie could hear her slamming the contents of the cupboard around. She twisted her hair around her first two fingers and tentatively ventured a comment.

"Well, he did steal your money..." Julie trailed off as Rosanna reappeared from under the bench, brandishing an enormous bottle of vodka.

"For emergencies only. I don't think a virgin smoothie is really gonna hit it tonight, do you?" Rosanna's eyes glittered wickedly and Julie saw she was in no mood for further discussion as she began to pour liberally into the blender.

"You sure you still want kids?"

"Oh sure." Julie couldn't tear her eyes away from the never-ending stream of alcohol.

Distracted, she didn't notice Rosanna shift the focus from her own domestic issues. "Just me and Roger have agreed to wait a little while longer, you know? He thinks it'd be good to wait and see if he gets this promotion."

Rosanna paused, finally setting the bottle down on the counter. Eventually she spoke. "Right."

Right? That was it, right? Mostly relieved, Julie breathed out as Rosanna poured the alco-smoothie into two tall glasses and tipped one back for a long sip.

A small part of Julie was disappointed she didn't get a chance to confide in her friend how disappointed she was that her long-planned baby was on hold – again – but, on the other hand, was she really in the mood for one of Rosanna's long diatribes on the failings of Roger? Maybe not...

"So," Rosanna broke into her thoughts, "It's your turn for movie night, what have you got?"

"What have I got?" All thoughts of Roger suddenly forgotten, Julie was up and dancing on the balls of her feet, excited like a child. "What have I got? Come with me!"

3

Slightly dubious, Rosanna trailed behind Julie as she practically skipped down to the Chili-mobile. Julie popped the trunk and a cloud of dust rose up to greet them.

Rosanna covered her drink with her hand – no point wasting good vodka, she thought. Or fruit. I mean, all those vitamins...

Oblivious to the dust cloud, Julie reached into the trunk and heaved up an enormous metal box, battered and scuffed but still recognizable as...

"A Betamax?" coughed Rosanna.

"Isn't it great? I found it clearing out Mom's garage after the funeral."

Rosanna was unimpressed. "You find a phonograph in there as well?"

"You know my mom. I certainly didn't find any family mementos. I guess she thought she might get a few dollars for this someday. Here, take it." She dumped the ancient VCR in Rosanna's arms and hauled out a box of tapes.

* * *

As Julie rummaged at the back of Rosanna's TV, hooking up the old Betamax, Rosanna was pulling tapes out of the box with glee.

"Oh God, *Pretty in Pink*. Who do you think you'd go for now – Andrew McCarthy or James Spader?"

Julie didn't even look up from behind the TV.

"Definitely Duckie."

"Duckie? Seriously? Duckie?"

This time Julie did look up, a little pink in the cheeks. "Yeah, when I was seventeen, I used to fantasize that he would cycle past my house, like, when I didn't see."

Rosanna wanted to laugh, but sometimes really, Julie was so sweet and innocent, she just couldn't poke fun at her. "Come on, get that hooked up and pick a tape. I'll go pour a couple more smoothies."

* * *

How could Rosanna have ever doubted Julie?

The carrot cake was amazing. Jon Cryer was still not sexy though, even this late and after so many alcosmoothies, Rosanna was starting to lose feeling in her lips. A lump of frosting slid down her chin and she caught it with her finger, quickly licking off every last crumb. "God, this cake is amazing."

Julie smiled with satisfaction. "It's the sweet chili sauce with the cream cheese. The cheese takes the heat out, so you just get the flavor." She looked back at the TV. "God, I will never understand why Andie goes back to Blane at the prom. Duckie loved her all that time and he was there for her, you know?"

"Oh no. No, no, no. I'm sorry honey, but we need to put this Team Duckie shit to bed once and for all."

"Duckie shit? Is that squishy?" Julie poked her tongue out and Rosanna could feel the heat rising. She had a very serious point to make, if she could just remember what it was. Oh yes.

"Look. Andie spends the whole movie – the *whole* movie – pining for this Blane guy. The whole movie is this star-crossed love story, where everyone's against them and then right at the end she's just gonna turn around and go, 'Oh sorry Blane, I know the whole point is that we're in love against the odds and all but, actually, I've just realized I'm in love with Duckie, who's been hanging around waiting for me the past eight years and I just never noticed before. Oops.'"

Rosanna saw Julie about to open her mouth to protest and cut her off. "No. No no no no no. Absolutely not. Just no."

Rosanna finally paused to take a long pull on her drink and Julie saw her opening.

"Okaaay. But it was so lame, that whole ending, like Duckie's been in love with Andie forever and then suddenly there's some cheesy blonde winking at him and he just forgets all about her."

Rosanna squinted at Julie through dirty blonde hair. "I'll give you that. So how would you have ended it?"

"Oh, I'd have saved Iona from pet store yuppie hell. She could have been his older woman, initiated him into the ways of love, broken his little heart and left him ready for the real love of his life."

"And who's that, you?"

Julie didn't answer, but a secret smile crept across her face as she took another sip of her drink.

"So," Rosanna broke across her reverie. "What's next, *The Sure Thing*?"

"Ooh, *The Sure Thing*, *The Sure Thing* – put it on!"

* * *

MUCH later, Gib snuck through the den, to see his mother and his Aunt Julie kneeling on the floor, each holding a can of beer and a pen. "You ready?" his mom asked Julie, oblivious to his presence. Then suddenly the two women violently stabbed the cans of beer, ripped the ring pulls and started chugging from the pen holes.

"Mom! What are you guys doing?" Beer sprayed everywhere as the two women turned to see Gib's outraged face. There was a horrified pause before Rosanna and Julie collapsed into giggles.

"Oh Gib," gasped Julie, "we're reliving our misspent youth. You wouldn't understand, you haven't, um, spent it yet."

"Not like my fifty bucks." Rosanna grabbed Julie's arms and they fell against each other, helpless with laughter. "Oh come on Gib, come join us for a beer. Gib."

Mutinously, Gib stared, refusing to answer. Rosanna held his gaze for a moment, then was distracted by something – John Cusack as Walter 'Gib' Gibson filled the screen, pining for Daphne Zuniga.

"Oh look, your namesake! He should have been your real father, you know."

As Gib stormed out in disgust, Rosanna licked frosting thoughtfully from her fingers. "You know, I think that's when I finally realized I was a grown-up."

"Really, that happened did it? When?"

Rosanna looked at the screen and sighed. "When I realized I really never was gonna marry John Cusack."

"Oh, I got over that when he took his shirt off in *High Fidelity*." Julie collapsed into giggles again. Out of the corner of her eye, she could see Rosanna's disapproval but hey, if she couldn't appreciate the Duckman, there was no helping her.

***

Blearily, Rosanna peered over the rim of her glass. She was awake, just about, but she could feel delicious, drunken sleep washing over her, pulling her under, mmmmm...

The only thing that was disturbing her slide into dreamland was Julie. What was she doing? She seemed to be frantically rummaging through the box of tapes, muttering to herself.

"Hah! Got it!"

Rosanna jolted fully awake. Kind of. "What?"

Julie was waving a home recording tape in the air. Dotted all over the handwritten label were little gold stars. "I found it, look." She handed the tape to Rosanna, who turned it over.

'If You Leave', read the label in black Sharpied capitals.

"Geez, I forgot all about this one." She looked up to see Julie buzzing.

"Remember when we watched this, like, every Friday night for three months?"

"No, that was just you."

Julie's face fell. "Oh yeah, you had a lot of dates."

"Geez, you make me sound like such a tramp. You were only at home because you had that totally obsessive crush on the main guy in this, what was his name?"

Rosanna threw the tape back at Julie, who deftly caught it. She turned to put it in the VCR. "I did not have a crush on him."

"You so did. Come on, who was the guy?"

Julie blushed, the tape in her hand hovering over the

Betamax. "It wasn't the main guy, it was the other guy, Johnnie, the one who's madly in love with her and she's totally oblivious. 'Cause she's an idiot."

"Hah!" Rosanna felt she'd scored her point. "And now you're totally perving over him all over again, you dirty old woman."

"I am not!" Julie grabbed a cushion and threw it at Rosanna's head, but Rosanna was suddenly sharp, awake again and hopping with devilment. She deftly caught the cushion and threw it back at Julie.

"You so are! Are you going to tell me if you had the chance to be eighteen again, you wouldn't still like him?"

Julie paused, "I don't know. I guess there's a part of your head that's always going to think you're still eighteen." She grinned, looking at her friend. "In your case, it's just a little overdeveloped." She turned again to the VCR and punched the eject button. The top loading deck popped up.

"Oh God, Ju, I don't think I can take any more. I'm gonna OD on nostalgia."

Julie turned to Rosanna with a beseeching smile. "Just this one more, please?"

Seeing Rosanna's face register defeat, Julie slid the tape into the deck, pressed it down and hopped up onto the couch to snuggle up next to her friend. She sighed with satisfaction as the studio ident appeared on the screen and the familiar images from a long time ago began to roll...

A mass of schoolkids, all different tribes, pour towards the front of Shermer High as another school day begins.

The camera closes in on three guys in supercool wraparound sunglasses. They look to their right in perfect synchronization to see...

...a VW camper van screech to a halt and three stoners fall out the side door in a cloud of smoke.

Meanwhile, in a bright and tidy suburban kitchen, a young girl with a mane of wiry blonde hair tears a bite out of a slice of toast as she grabs her school bag and heads for the door. She calls out, "Bye Dad, gotta motor!"

Her father - a stocky, cheerful man in his early fifties, dressed neatly in a short-sleeve check shirt and dark pants – grabs her by the shoulders and kisses her on the cheek. "You ready for your big day, sweetheart?"

"I know Dad, because every day's a big day." She smiles wryly, but there's real affection there. She turns to go, but he doesn't let go her shoulders until she gives him a big kiss on the cheek. "Dad, I gotta go!"

* * *

The scene cuts to another kitchen, but a much more chintzy number this time. A second young girl dressed in midnight blue silk pajamas, her dark hair scraped up in a high ponytail, sits open-mouthed at the table as her mother places in front of her the world's biggest stack of pancakes, dripping in syrup.
As the dark-haired girl looks up at her adoring mom... BANG! They both whip round to see a ten year old boy fly backward through the air and slam into the wall behind them.

The boy picks himself up, pushes back his plastic protective goggles, dusts off his soot-soiled lab coat and strides back towards the source of the explosion. Mom smiles indulgently.

Back in reality, Julie sighed. "Ohhh, I used to wish so much that she was my mom."

Before her brain had a chance to engage, Rosanna's mouth was open. "If I'd had your mom, I'd wish Freddy Kreuger was my mom." Seeing Julie flinch, she instantly regretted the stupid wisecrack. "Sorry, she's dead now. I should shut up."

Rosanna could have bitten her tongue out as pain flitted across Julie's face. "No, it's okay... Well, it's not okay, but it's alright. You know what I mean."

"I know what you mean, honey."

Rosanna drew her old friend's head onto her shoulder and stroked her hair like a small child's as they settled down to watch the rest of the film. God, it was nice to watch all these old movies together, if only she could keep her eyes open. She was gonna regret that last alco-smoothie in the morning...

* * *

As the women slept, the film played on:

An eighties prom scene fills the screen, one heaving mass of shot taffeta, puffball sleeves, silver Lurex and home perms. A giant net full of balloons waits to open from the ceiling.

At the still center of the frantic dancefloor are a young couple – the girl with the wiry blonde hair and a boy. His name is Andrew. He looks a lot like a young John Cusack.

From the side of the dancefloor, Johnnie - a sweet, geeky boy in the 'Duckie' mold - gazes at the couple forlornly, then turns and runs from the hall.

As the couple turns slowly, Andrew holds her a little closer. "It's okay if you don't believe in me, but I need you to believe in you." He holds the girl's gaze for a long moment as her eyes fill with tears.

"And you think a stupid video can just fix everything?"

Behind them, above the stage where the band play, is a large screen on which a home video is playing. It's edited like a music video, with shots of the girl with wiry hair laughing, running, falling into swimming pools. It's a love letter to her smile. It's the video we might have wished our favorite pop star would make of us, when we were teenage girls.

She pulls out of his embrace and runs to the side of the stage, through a red curtain. Behind the curtain is a VCR.

Dodging behind the curtain, she lunges at the VCR, jamming buttons, getting more and more frantic in her distress as she tries to eject the tape.

* * *

On the screen, the tracking began to strobe. A strange ripping noise came from the VCR as Julie and Rosanna snoozed on, oblivious, until...

BANG! Both women jumped a clear foot off of the couch as smoke began to pour from the Betamax. Julie was first to shake off her slumber. "Oh no, my tape!"

She grabbed a cake fork from her plate and lunged for the top loading deck.

Coming to, Rosanna realized what Julie was doing. "Stop!" She grabbed Julie's arm, just as the world seemed to explode around them in a blinding flash of light.

Then all was darkness.

Darkness and silence...

4

Rosanna was the first to wake up. Soft, dusty light filtered in through pink chiffon sheers at the window. She looked around. Where was Julie? As she clutched her pounding head, she realized that Julie's absence wasn't the only strange thing going on here.

Where was she? She was in bed, but not her bed. Definitely not some random guy's either.

All around her was a miasma of pink: pink floral wallpaper lined the walls; every piece of furniture was draped with pink scarves, pink summer hats, pink kimonos - it was like Barbie had barfed Pepto Bismol all over her dream house.

Rosanna's stomach clenched and rolled.

***

Meanwhile, Julie was waking up to her own nightmare. Posters for The Cure, Simple Minds, Cabaret Voltaire and The Smiths leered at her from every inch of available wall space.

She looked down at her hands – her wedding rings were gone. Come to think of it, these didn't even look like her hands. *How much had she had to drink last night?* There must be something wrong with her eyes.

Getting out of the strange bed, she stumbled to the dresser and blinked up at the mirror.

Blinking back at her was a young girl in a neat pair of midnight blue silk pajamas, a ponytail tied high on her head.

* * *

Across town, Rosanna looked in the pink-framed mirror on the pink dresser. Looking back at her was a young girl with wiry blonde hair falling into her eyes.

If the girls had been nearer each other, they would at that moment have heard the other SCREAM!

5

In a daze, Rosanna stumbled out of the pink room.

A stocky, cheerful familiar figure, in his early fifties, hurried out of the bathroom and came across the hall to plant a kiss on her forehead. "Don't be late honey, big day at school today."

Rosanna shrank against the wall, pulling her pink robe tight. "Big day?"

Her 'Dad' bustled on down the stairs, calling behind him, "Sure. Every day's a big day if you treat it like one."

* * *

In a daze, Julie stumbled out of her room.

A gorgeous nineteen year old blonde was banging on the bathroom door. Totally ignoring Julie, she hollered down the stairs. "MOOOOM! He's been in there forever and I have to pee!" Smoke and flashes of green light appeared from under the locked door. Totally stunned, Julie headed downstairs.

Through the third door she tried was a homey, chintzy kitchen. It was the best smelling kitchen she had ever been in. The thought crossed her mind that Martha Stewart would go back to jail to make her house smell this fresh-baked.

The word *pancakes* registered in the back of her mind and then suddenly, standing right in front of her, was the woman she'd always dreamed would be her ideal mom.

Her 'mom's' arms opened to her. "Maple or blueberry, Honey?"

Of course, Julie thought as she let herself be enfolded in a warm, sweet-smelling embrace. Of course, I'm having a dream. Hope I don't wake up anytime soon.

Relaxing into the warm, comforting dream, Julie let her 'Mom' lead her to the kitchen table, where the world's biggest stack of pancakes, drowning in syrup, appeared in front of her.

Across the table, her 'Dad' lowered his newspaper and took the pipe out of his mouth. "Morning, Pumpkin."

* * *

Stepping off the yellow school bus, Rosanna stopped dead, oblivious to the shoving and complaints of the kids getting off behind her. Dumbstruck, she saw...

A mass of schoolkids, all different tribes, pouring towards the front of Shermer High for the start of another school day.

Three guys in supercool wraparound sunglasses, looking to their right in perfect synchronization to see...

...a VW camper van screech to a halt and three stoners fall out the side door in a cloud of smoke.

Then a red Ferrari pulled up behind the VW van and a boy in a trench coat, sunglasses and an old-man hat got out.

As a teenage couple pushed past her, hands in each other's back jeans pockets, Rosanna started to shake herself out of it and as she did, she noticed another young girl standing staring at the scene in front of them. A girl with dark hair in a high ponytail.

A couple of tendrils had escaped the ponytail and the girl was twisting them around her first two fingers in an anxious gesture that was so familiar...

"Julie?"

Ponytail jumped about a foot in the air.

"Julie, is that you?"

Julie turned around. "Rosanna?"

"What is going—?"

Her sentence was cut short as a cute and slightly nervous boy, his hair swept up into a teddy boy quiff, rushed up to them.

"Johnnie," breathed Julie.

But he didn't even see her. "Hey Rosanna, hey, what's up? You're looking stunning, as ever." Finally, he saw Julie. "Oh, hi Julie."

But then, as Julie silently deflated, he stopped and looked at her again. "Julie, you look different today. Is something different?"

"No, what...?" Realization dawned. "Did you just call me Julie?"

As Julie stood, stunned, Johnnie clasped her hand and swept into a low bow. "Why of course, I forgot, I should call you Duchess! Principessa." He kissed her hand, looking up at her with a look of pure mischief. "Milady."

Was he flirting with her? For a moment Julie held her breath, then the moment was gone as he spotted Rosanna walking towards the school and dropped Julie's hand like a stone to give chase. "Rosanna, hey, wait up!"

Julie sighed.

* * *

Everything was too much as the girls stumbled down the busy school hallway, folders clutched close to their chests for the illusion of protection.

Teenagers everywhere were slouching, leaning, laughing, talking, sizing each other up. Some looked daggers at Julie and Rosanna as they walked past, others were coolly assessing in their gaze.

Hand-painted banners hung from the ceiling: *Vote for your Prom King and Queen; Go Wolves!*

Oblivious to the girls' confusion, Johnnie was giving a running commentary on everyone and everything.

"Well ladies, it's another fulfilling day of higher education. On your right, you'll see our resident beautiful people..."

Trailing behind him, Julie and Rosanna looked dazedly to the right, to see a crowd of rich preppies in expensive pastel linens, cream sweaters tied around their shoulders, sneering back at them.

"And if you look to your left, our football team is just warming up for a day of intellectual and athletic endeavor."

Swinging obediently to the left, the girls saw a bunch of jocks trying to stuff a much smaller boy into a locker.

Behind them, a girl in a neck brace was trying - and failing - to drink from the water fountain.

"Here we have our motorheads, our geeks, the sluts, wastoids, dweebies..."

Rosanna felt her head swim as all the teenage faces started to blur into one. Then she noticed Johnnie suddenly stop.

Looking from his confused face to the boy across the hall, she too stopped still. It was *HIM*, the John-Cusack-a-like romantic lead, her all-time teen movie crush, Andrew. Leaning against the lockers, cooler than cool, as if he were real or something.

Vaguely, she heard Johnnie start to speak again. "Well here's a totally new face. Stay tuned for further developments."

Behind Johnnie, Julie mouthed along with his words. She'd seen this scene so many times before; the craziness was building in her head like steam and it felt like she was about to blow.

Seeing Rosanna transfixed, and seeing the girl's bathroom door behind her, Julie took her chance and grabbed Rosanna, hustling her bodily into the bathroom.

Flying through the door, Julie landed against Rosanna as they slammed into the stall door opposite. Not even pausing to stand up straight, Julie started to scream.

"What is going on here?"

"I have no idea. Is this real? Are *you* real?" Rosanna pinched Julie, hard.

"Ow!" Julie rubbed her arm, temporarily distracted from her mounting hysteria. "Claws off, Mr. Krabs. Pinch yourself!"

She pinched Rosanna, who straightaway pinched her back. As the pinch-off degenerated into slapping, Julie grabbed Rosanna by the hair.

"Ow, ow, ow, okay! Stop, okay!" Extremely painfully, Rosanna managed to straighten up and take Julie by the shoulders, looking her in the eye.

As Julie began to calm down. Rosanna kept a hold of her shoulders, held her gaze and started to talk veeerrry calmly.

"Now this is obviously just a really weird dream. I don't know if it's yours yet, or if it's mine, but it's got to be a dream."

Julie's breathing began to slow and she loosened her grip on Rosanna's hair. "You think it's just a dream?"

Relaxing, Rosanna let go her friend's shoulders. "Well yeah, of course. And this could be a pretty damn good dream. I mean, he's here. Really, really here. And in this movie he's mine, right?"

Nursing her jaw, which still smarted from a particularly hard slap, Julie looked up at her friend and felt her disbelief turn to sudden anger. "Unbelievable. We're in my dream, *my* favorite movie and I'm here as the sidekick."

Sensing her friend's anger, Rosanna backed away a little before she asked her next question. "How do you know it's your dream?"

BANG! Cutting off this thought, a hot blonde girl in top-to-toe pink spandex slammed her way out of the middle stall, stubbed a cigarette on the side of the door and headed for the washbasins to give her hands a cursory shake under the faucet.

How long had she been there?

"You two are so incredibly weird." Too long, obviously. The blonde rolled her eyes and headed for the door, leaving Julie and Rosanna alone again. Slightly chastened, Julie looked to Rosanna. "So, what do we do now."

"Well, till we figure this out... I guess we go to class."

"I don't know if I'm emotionally ready."

* * *

As Julie and Rosanna tentatively pushed open a classroom door, a formidable, willowy, gray-haired woman paced the front of the room.

"This week's assignment is to rewrite last week's assignment."

The class groaned as one as she continued to speak in a husky Swedish accent, everything she said punctuated with swoops and flourishes of her expressive hands.

Spotting Johnnie at the back of the class, Julie shoved Rosanna, and every head turned as the two girls burst into the classroom.

"Sorry we're late," ventured Rosanna.

"Yeah." After shoving her, Julie felt she really should back Rosanna up. "Um, there was this thing and we're late because of it." Well, she tried.

The teacher raised her eyebrows high into her hairline and the girls braced themselves for a verbal lashing, but she was obviously having a good day - waving the girls to two empty seats, she continued to berate the rest of the class.

Johnnie turned round from his seat in front of Julie. "Where were you guys?"

Shit! Julie's brain whirred in confusion, but the classroom door opened again and it was all eyes front as Andrew appeared, ushered in by a distracted-looking middle aged man in a tweed jacket with suede elbow patches.

The man cleared his throat loudly. Thus prompted, the class spoke as one. "Good morning, Mr. Donnelly."

"Class, today we welcome a new student. Andrew is joining us from Berryman High where he, er, left."

Clearing his throat again, Mr. Donnelly made an abrupt exit, leaving Andrew stranded at the front of the classroom.

As he slid into a seat near the front, Rosanna stared at him, lost in reverie until she was distracted by a very unsubtle tap on her shoulder. The girl behind her leaned forward and whispered excitedly. "I heard he got kicked out of his last school for setting fire to the gym."

Really? thought Rosanna. Andrew was even more interesting than she remembered...

* * *

In the yard after class, Andrew's history grew more lurid as each student seemed to have a rumor to add to the pile. Even Johnnie had heard something, "I heard it was because he had sex with his Chem teacher."

A geeky boy broke in, almost choking with excitement, "No, I heard it was the Principal's wife!"

Rosanna was only half-listening as she watched Andrew across the yard. He could be watching her right back, but with dark glasses covering his eyes as he slouched against a sunny wall, it was hard to tell.

He slowly took the glasses off, like he was asking a question and started to walk towards her.

Panicked, Rosanna became aware that the geeky boy was still telling his story. "They had to break it off when he was arrested for making LSD in his mom's basement. He was supplying the entire North-Eastern region..."

"See?" Johnnie interrupted, "That's how you know it was his Chem teacher. That's how he got the formulas to..."

"To what?" It was Johnnie's turn to be interrupted as

Andrew joined the excitable group under the tree. Lucky for Johnnie, Andrew wasn't that interested. Ignoring the rest of the group, he turned straight to Rosanna.

"You wanna go someplace tonight?"

"Sure." Too shocked to say anymore, Rosanna watched as he walked away, cool as anything.

Then turned on his heel and walked straight back.

"Ah, that went a lot better in my head. What I meant to say is can I meet you somewhere? Is there a place we should go? Is there a time I can pick you up?"

Rosanna's shock melted as she saw his awkwardness. Okay, so he wasn't Mr. Supercool, but this was a lot less intimidating. "How about my house? Seven o'clock? I'll text..."

Patting her pocket, it was Rosanna's turn to be flustered as she realized not only did she not have her smartphone, but it wouldn't be invented for another decade or so.

And not only that, but she had no idea where she lived or how to get there. "Hang on."

Pulling Julie to one side, she whispered furiously. "Jules, where do I live?"

Julie looked at her, stunned. "I don't know!"

"I thought you knew this movie backward?" Glancing over nervously, Rosanna saw Andrew hold his hands up, a questioning look on his face.

"I didn't memorize it!" As she got more upset, Julie's voice started to rise. "Anyway, you can't go on a date, we have to get home."

Ignoring her distress, Rosanna spun Julie around and started rummaging through her backpack. "Is there anything in your bag? A letter? A note?"

Oblivious to the growing stares of the rest of the group, Rosanna tossed tissues, lipsticks, Sharpies to the ground.

"Ha!" She brandished a small, leather-bound address book. "Even your alter-ego is organized." Scanning quickly, she found her name in small, neat script above an address.

Taking a deep breath and trying hard to zone out her awareness of what a giant weirdo she must look, she did her best to memorize the details. Then, dropping the address book back in Julie's bag, she picked up a sharpie from the ground and walked back to Andrew.

Avoiding his eye, she wrote her address neatly on Andrew's arm. "Just had to check my, ah, my schedule."

"And is your friend letting you out to play?" Looking up at last, her eyes met his, warm and amused.

"Just pick me up at seven, okay?" She smiled back, feeling the connection between them, natural as honey.

He started to walk away, backing off, not breaking eye contact. "Well let me know if any wrinkles appear in your schedule." Turning at last, he called back over his shoulder, "Or your PA could call me."

Stunned, Johnnie stared forlornly at Rosanna, as she watched Andrew walk away. "She's going on a date? With that guy? Did she just do that?"

Julie patted him on the shoulder. "She was always going to do that." Oblivious to her kindness, Johnnie drifted over to Rosanna.

Julie sighed. No one noticed.

6

By pure luck, Rosanna managed to remember some of the faces from that morning's bus ride. Well, not so much the faces as the jock straps worn upside down on the heads of two bespectacled boys, who leered over the seats at Julie and Rosanna for the whole journey home, suggestively stroking their large, plastic water pistols. Who was gonna forget these guys?

Rosanna leaned over to Julie and whispered out the side of her mouth, eyes fixed on the Jock-Strap Twins to make sure there were no sudden moves. "Why didn't our characters ever learn to drive?"

So they were probably on the right bus but still, how would they ever know which stop was theirs? After a half hour of restlessly scanning every house they passed, Julie realized that the bus driver was yelling at them. Well, at Rosanna.

"Peterson. Hey, Peterson! You gonna hold up the bus all day or are you gonna get off?" Falling off the bus, almost crying with relief, the girls stumbled up the driveway and found that the key in Rosanna's pocket fitted the door.

When they got into the house, it was mercifully empty – Rosanna's 'Dad' must be still at work.

After trying the first few doors upstairs, they found the shrine-to-pink that was now Rosanna's bedroom. As Rosanna disappeared into the closet to find a perfect outfit, Julie sank into the marshmallow bed, grateful to have finally made it there.

Then just as she started to relax, a fresh realization hit her – how would she find her own 'home'? And what about her real home?

Rosanna was focusing on the really important things though. Turning round and round, she admired her brand new body in the closet mirror. "Look at my butt." She patted it proudly with both hands. "I love my eighteen year old butt!"

Julie didn't even hear her. "God Rosanna, what are we going to do?"

"Do? I'm gonna wear the tightest pants I can find – this is amazing!"

"No Rosanna, what are we doing here? None of this makes any sense."

Ignoring her friend's concerns, Rosanna stuck her head back in the closet. "Why are you trying to make sense of it? It's obviously a dream. We're not here."

Julie wanted to believe it, to be as confident and relaxed as Rosanna, but she just couldn't let it go. She pulled a tendril of hair around her fingers.

"Well, it's not like any dream I ever had. This feels *super*-real. Last thing I remember was, I stuck my fork in that stupid VCR and something went bang..."

She stopped, feeling all the blood drain from her heart. "What if we're dead?"

"Hnfh?" Rosanna couldn't say she was really listening. She'd found a topless black boater hat in the top of the closet and she was busy fixing her hair to cascade over the top, mouth full of about a hundred hair pins. The word 'dead' had got her attention though.

"What if we're dead and this is the afterlife?" Julie was getting really worked up now.

"What if we're trapped in an eighties teen movie for all eternity? I mean, did we do good or did we do bad to end up here?"

"Well, if we're dead, we can't do a whole lot about it, can we?" Rosanna appeared from behind the closet door again, in head to toe marble-wash stretch denim. Seeing Julie's face, she figured the outfit was not a hit and disappeared back into the closet.

"Well okay, what if we're not dead, but this is some kind of weird coma dream that we're both having and any minute now we're going to look down and see ourselves in adjoining beds, with backless gowns and drool coming out of our mouths."

Rosanna appeared again, resplendent in head-to-toe clashing neons, complete with lime green legwarmers and orange stilettos. Even in the midst of her misery, Julie winced, but then started to look close to tears again.

Seeing her friend genuinely upset, Rosanna tore herself away from the closet and knelt down to look Julie in the eye. She took her gently by the shoulders.

"Hey honey, it's okay. We're not dead, and we're not in a coma. This is just some crazy dream. Some crazy, really, really, long and super-realistic dream."

Rosanna shook herself. She couldn't start going down Julie's rabbit hole of hysteria. "It's not so bad. I'm going on my dream date; you're living in your Barbie dream house with your ideal mom. Let's just enjoy it till we wake up."

Just thinking about her movie mom made Julie feel a little warmer, safer. It was nice to be in that house, where everything was just how she'd dreamed a family should be, growing up.

Every room smelled like fresh-baked bread or cut flowers; people argued and fell out, but they fundamentally loved each other to bits; and no one was gonna wake you up at two a.m. and make you stand shivering in your nightgown for three hours, while they bawled you out for forgetting to tape Cheers.

Seeing Julie lost in a happy reverie, Rosanna got back down to the serious business of selecting a super-hot outfit. But something was niggling at her now. "Did we ever find out, in the movie, why Andrew did get kicked out of school?"

"No, don't you remember?" Julie knew that was a redundant question – she didn't even know if Rosanna had seen the whole thing through once, never mind as many times as she had, but she certainly didn't mind recalling the whole romantic story. "That was the end of the movie - after she...well, *you* get electrocuted, he brings you round with a kiss and then she asks him again what happened. He's just about to tell her, and it cuts to black. Y'know, finito, credits roll..."

Julie looked up to see Rosanna bearing down upon her, in a short white lace dress, a large *BoyToy* pendant on a chain around her neck. Distracted by the outfit, she didn't see the murderous light in Rosanna's eye.

"Did you just say electrocuted?"

"You gonna wear that, really?" Seeing Rosanna raise her eyebrows through her hairline, Julie realized she hadn't answered the question. "Oh yeah, electrocuted, you remember, at the Prom?"

Rosanna put her face right up to Julie's, desperate to get her to focus now. "Jules, you watched this movie seventy thousand times, not me. What happens at the Prom?"

Julie saw that Rosanna was serious, but she couldn't work out why. What was the big deal with the Prom? "Oh, well, you're there with Johnnie."

"Why am I there with Johnnie?"

"Well you and Andrew have a fight, 'cause of your scholarship."

Rosanna felt her temples start to ache. "What scholarship? Ju, I think you need to go back a bit."

Rosanna's mind was racing in a thousand possible directions, but she still needed to focus on the important things. Hot date. Hot outfit. As she listened to Julie, she dove back into the closet.

"Okay." Julie took a deep breath and began. "You get offered a scholarship to this really great art school. In Paris."

Rosanna reappeared in candy pink baggy overalls and a high-necked pink and white striped shirt. "Remind me again why we're so desperate to get out of here."

Julie grimaced – at Rosanna *and* her clothes. "Shut up, I'm thinking. Right, so it's totally your dream, you've got to go to Paris. So you break up with Andrew, and you agree to go to the Prom with Johnnie, 'cause he's been in love with you, just, forever."

Curious, Rosanna appeared again in a bright blue skirt suit. "He has? Really?"

Julie bristled. "Yeah, but not really an important detail. What is that outfit all about?"

Rosanna looked down. "Too demure."

"You look like Lady Di. And how are you even getting changed so fast?"

Nonplussed, Rosanna disappeared again. "I dunno –

I don't even remember putting these clothes on." Emerging from the closet a second later, she shook herself. "Right, so we're at the Prom?"

"Well no, first we go shopping for dresses. Oh my God, your dress is amaaaaazing!"

"Like you said Jules, not really an important detail. Come on, we're at the Prom, so how does this thing end?"

"Stop rushing me! We're at the Prom..."

"I think we established we're at the Prom."

"We're at the Prom and Andrew plays this video he's made of you. It's like you, and everything about you, set to music. Oh God, it's so romantic..."

Rosanna could see she was losing Julie again. "So what, we get back together and live happily ever after in Paris?"

"Yes!" Julie cried. "Well no. Not yet. See, you're all upset and you go to grab the tape out of the machine, but you get an electric shock and..."

BAM! Julie's mouth opened in shock as Rosanna bounded across the room and slapped her HARD across the face. Shocked, she barely even took in the combination of a plum-colored tube top and a frontless, backless gray unitard that Rosanna was wearing.

"Are you kidding me?" Rosanna screamed. "Did you just say I get electrocuted at the Prom?"

Julie rubbed her flaming cheek. "Well, yeah..."

"By a VCR?"

"Yeah." Light was beginning to dawn at the back of Julie's mind; there was something Rosanna was getting at if she could just grasp it...

"And there's nothing going on in that great big

movie-nut brain of yours, no connection, no thoughts about how we got here in the first place?"

"Ohhhhh." The dawn in Julie's mind was suddenly a bright burst of sunshine – she'd been so stupid! "Oh shit, we could..." Looking up, she saw Rosanna nodding slowly at her, waiting for her to get all caught up. "We can go home! Oh God!"

"Yes!" And Rosanna was up and pacing the room. "See, that must be it! It's easy. All we got to do is sit tight till the end of the week, get to Prom and stick a fork in a VCR."

Calm and energized, she turned back to the mirror and started applying lipstick.

Julie still sat paralyzed on the bed, struggling to get her head around the implications. "But we can't just stay here for a week. What about Roger?"

Rosanna didn't even turn around – she wasn't worried about how a grown man was going to look after himself.

Julie tried another tack. "What about Gib?"

Rosanna paused, lipstick hovering over her mouth. But no, nothing was going to kill her buzz here. "Gib, it'd do him good to miss me. Roger too. Maybe they'll appreciate us more."

Julie reeled - how could she be so blasé? "I can't believe you're going on a date and leaving me here. And it's not even real!"

Rosanna couldn't take this anymore. Turning, she grabbed Julie and shook her by the shoulders fiercely. "You're right. It's not real. So why are you taking it so seriously? God, there are no consequences here. Don't you get it? This is a dream, it's a fantasy, we can do anything we want. And I want to enjoy it! What do you want? Think about it, Julie."

As Rosanna turned angrily back to the mirror to start applying the first of five shades of eyeshadow, Julie was lost in thought. What did she want? It was so long since she'd allowed herself to contemplate it and now here? In this place? What could she possibly want here…?

But no, she couldn't think about that. This was ridiculous. She was a grown woman with a good life: steady job (maybe); loving husband (kind of); and… well, she still had all her own teeth and that's not bad. There was no way she was going to act like Rosanna, chasing after some guy she'd been in love with since she was eighteen the first time around…

Julie's train of thought was interrupted by a knock at the bedroom door. A head appeared around the door. "Hi girls, all ready for the big night?"

Julie couldn't believe it. I mean obviously, in this movie, this was his house, and she'd met a lot of fictional people today, but it was still a shock, seeing Rosanna's 'Dad' right in front of her, talking to her, like this was real life.

Then she realized he was looking at her, waiting for a response. "Oh, hi Mr. Peterson."

His face broke into an avuncular smile. "I've told you before, Julie, call me Bob."

"Really? Oh, I mean yes, sure Bob." Julie didn't know how much longer she could keep up the appearance of normalcy, but then all at once Mr. Peterson's attention was on Rosanna and, more to the point, on her outfit.

He looked her up and down and the smile curdled on his face. "So where are you girls going tonight?"

Oblivious to her 'Dad's' disapproving looks, Rosanna was still doing her make-up. "Well actually, I have a date."

"A date?" Mr. Peterson's smile drew a couple of notches tighter.

"Yeah, a big date. He's picking me up at seven."

Mr. Peterson looked like he was getting a serious case of cheek-ache. "Who's picking you up? Have I met this boy?"

Still not meeting his eye, Rosanna fluffed her hair in the mirror, bigger and bigger. "Um no, he's new at school. Had to transfer out of the last one because his grades were just too high and he was way too popular."

"Well that... Well that sounds nice, honey." Mr. Peterson began to recover himself, but he looked confused. "You double dating tonight, Julie?"

"No, I'm uh..." Now it was Julie's turn to be confused. What was she gonna do? What should she tell Mr. Peterson?

But she was saved by the bell – the doorbell. As Mr. Peterson went to go answer it, Julie grabbed Rosanna, frantic now with worry. "Rosanna, what am I gonna do tonight? How do I even get home?"

"Like I said, Jules, we can do anything we want." Rosanna kissed Julie on the cheek, leaving a smear of jammy lipstick and pulled her out into the hall, to lean over the top of the stairs.

***

The girls watched through the banisters as Andrew attempted to win over a stony-faced Mr. Peterson. He still hadn't gotten through the front door.

"Look, ah, I know you're busy, you don't have to entertain me, but you can trust me."

Still nothing from Mr. Peterson. Julie winced as Andrew started to babble nervously.

"So, I'll tell you a couple of things about myself. I'm an athlete, so I rarely drink. Kickboxing! You heard of kickboxing, sport of the future? I can see by your face, no."

Rosanna could see where this was going. More than that, she suddenly remembered where this was going and ran down the stairs to save Andrew from himself. Grabbing him by the arm, she sailed out the door, pulling Andrew with her and calling over her shoulder:

"His point is, Dad, you can relax and I'll be safe for the next seven to eight hours, okay? Love you, see you later." She turned back for just a second to plant a kiss on her 'Dad's' cheek and then steamed down the driveway to Andrew's beat up Oldsmobile, parked at the curb.

***

From the bedroom window, Julie watched forlornly as Rosanna ran laughing down the driveway, Andrew trailing in her wake. It was just like Rosanna to dive straight into this crazy situation and make the most of it, unafraid of anything. Well, maybe not so much like Rosanna lately, but a Rosanna she remembered from a long time ago.

As she pondered the dangerous implications of a Rosanna not just restored to a teenage body, but to her teenage self, she watched Andrew's car pull away and disappear around the corner.

As the noisy exhaust of the Oldsmobile died away in

the distance, a lone figure emerged from the shadows, riding a bicycle. He stopped and stared down the street in the direction Rosanna and Andrew had been just moments before. Julie could hear his heart breaking from the house.

She hesitated a moment and then slipped down the stairs and out onto the darkening street.

7

Johnnie rode his bike in disconsolate circles round and round, in the middle of the empty street.

Julie's ballet flats made no sound as she softly crossed the lawn, out onto the sidewalk. She watched Johnnie a moment more, unsure how or if she should make herself known.

Making a decision, she stepped out under a streetlight. Johnnie stopped his circling and – realizing who it was – tried to force some of his usual facade of good humor.

"Hey, it's Julie!"

Should she go along with his charade, let him save a little face? What the hell, Julie decided if she couldn't be herself, she might as well be herself. "Hey Johnnie, she break your heart again?"

Johnnie reddened, stumbled over his words. "What? I mean what? No! No, she'll come around. All the ladies do. She just hasn't realized yet that she's madly in love with me."

"Sure." Julie didn't trust herself to say any more. Then an idea struck her. "While you're waiting, can you... uh, you wanna walk me home?"

Johnnie patted the long seat of his chopper. "Sure. You wanna drive by the Snack Shack? Pick up some corn nuts?"

Julie smiled. "Well, if you're gonna be nice, I'll let you buy me a slushie."

"Cherry or cola?"

Julie didn't answer, but swung her leg over the chopper seat behind Johnnie. He pulled her arm around his waist. "You should hold on tight there." As he turned to catch Julie's eye, he blushed, suddenly very aware of their physical proximity. Julie smiled, and he relaxed and turned back towards the road.

Starting to pedal, Johnnie wobbled from the unfamiliar extra weight, but evened out as he picked up speed. Julie began to relax against the warmth of his back, stifling a sigh of satisfaction.

* * *

Meanwhile, Rosanna followed Andrew as he picked his way across the manicured golf course of what seemed to Rosanna to be an extremely swanky country club. In the distance, the clubhouse was lit up like Christmas and she could hear glasses clinking. If this was where they were going, was there a chance in hell of getting served at this bar? Was that why Andrew was taking her there?

She looked across at Andrew. In scruffy jeans and jacket, with a large backpack slung across his back, he didn't exactly look country club-ready. She grabbed his arm to get his attention. "Hey! I know you said it would be a surprise, but you're taking me to the country club? Seriously?"

"Sshhh! No, not exactly." Andrew shook off her arm as Rosanna attempted to ask again, "But..." He waved his hand down and put his finger to his lips, frantically signaling her to shut up as they approached the clubhouse.

Tiptoeing now, and more confused than ever,

Rosanna peered through the windows to see the well-dressed people inside. She could see a lot of hairspray and a *lot* of gold Lurex. Geez, she thought, why is it always the people who should least be seen in Lurex...

Suddenly she realized that Andrew was gone. She glanced around and, out of the corner of her eye, spotted a figure climbing the drainpipe of a small dark building with high brick walls and no windows.

"Andrew!" she whispered as loud as she dared as he disappeared over the top of the wall. "Andrew?"

As she stared up at the empty wall, she heard her name, "Rosanna! Over here."

Scanning down the wall, down, down, down, she saw him. He'd opened a door from inside and was beckoning her. "Come on, before someone sees us!"

* * *

As Rosanna entered, Andrew led her down a dark corridor and around a corner. In the dim light, she could just about make out rows of seats, like bleachers and then Andrew flipped a switch and she gasped as shimmering light bounced off the blue water and pale blue walls of an open air swimming pool – it was magical.

"Oh!" she gasped. "I don't remember... I mean, I didn't know you could get in here."

As she gazed around, enchanted, Andrew was busy unpacking the large backpack. He pulled out a rug from the top and laid it out by the pool. "It's alright," he reassured her, "no one ever uses this place at night."

Seeing her looking a little dazed, her led her to the rug and sat her down. Then she watched as he unpacked strawberries, bread, cheese... "Champagne?" She laughed.

He grinned back. "Seven dollars a bottle – the best in JJ's Stop 'n' Shop."

She accepted the plastic beaker he held out. "Well, this is all very romantic. What else have you got in there?" She reached into the bag and pulled out a pack of Twinkies. "Twinkies? Really?"

Andrew wasn't fazed. "That's one of your major food groups, right there. And if there's a nuclear war, it's the only foodstuff that'll survive."

Rosanna smiled wryly. "Well, I guess the cockroaches have to eat something."

"Not if I eat them first," said Andrew as he whipped the wrappers off two Twinkies and stuffed them both in his mouth. His cheeks bulged like a crazy hamster as he leaned in for a kiss.

Rosanna leaned back, laughing. "That is very attractive." He bent closer and closer to her, struggling to hold the Twinkies in when suddenly they heard a noise.

Rosanna and Andrew froze as footsteps echoed from the changing rooms.

* * *

As the black-clad security guard swung into the pool area, everything was silent. He looked around – he was sure he'd heard something and he was sick of local kids breaking in here, going skinny dipping and trashing the place. One of these days he'd catch them and....

Breaking off from happy thoughts of beatings and no witnesses, he realized the lights were on. Switching them off he turned to walk away. Wait! Did he hear something?

He swung his flashlight back, taking in every corner of the enclosure once, twice, then turned to go with a satisfied sneer. *Not on his watch, ha*!

The heavy footsteps faded away to nothing and all was completely still, until, until...

SPLASH! Heaving, spluttering, Andrew and Rosanna burst from the water, fully-clothed. As they gratefully gulped down lungfuls of air, Andrew let go the rug that their picnic was wrapped in. Plastic glasses, soggy bread rolls and bright-colored bags of chips floated up around them.

Starting to laugh, they clung to each other and, as the heaving gasps and the laughter subsided they locked eyes, suddenly aware they were in each other's arms.

Oblivious now to their wet clothes and ruined picnic, they melted together into one hot kiss.

Feeling a plastic packet bump her cheek, Rosanna broke off and looked around. "Do you think Twinkies can survive chlorinated water?"

Andrew looked down at the little floating packages and smiled, but he had too much sense to answer. He leaned in and kissed her again and this time she forgot everything.

8

Julie woke up. The phone next to her bed was ringing. Groggily, she reached one hand out from beneath the sheets. Something occurred to her, what was it? Oh yeah. That didn't sound like her phone...

Sitting bolt upright, she grabbed the handset and pulled it to her ear. "We're still here."

"I know!" Rosanna sang from the other end of the line, "Isn't it great!"

Rosanna had woken with the larks and was already showered, dressed and sitting at her dressing table, chunky cordless phone in one hand as her other was occupied trying on half a dozen hats in the mirror. She was buzzing!

Getting no response from Julie, she charged on. "So, I'm thinking, don't we skip school at some point in this movie?" She put down the hats and moved to the wardrobe, riffling through and discarding lacy tops, lacy skirts, lacy trousers...

"Wrong movie, Ro." Julie's head ached from trying to work it all out this early in the morning. "I think we should stick to the script. We only have to make it to Friday."

"Julie, seriously, come on." Rosanna was dangerously exuberant. "You already graduated high school once, you don't have to do it again!"

She tapped her fingers on the side of the closet, waiting for Julie to respond. Nothing.

Well, this will get a response, she thought. "I bet

Johnnie will come." She waited just a beat and then...

"I'll be at your house at eight."

Bingo! Rosanna hung up before Julie could change her mind again. Julie was too sensible for her own good and Rosanna was going to make sure she enjoyed this, this...whatever it was if it killed her!

* * *

Julie stumbled downstairs after her shower. What had she been thinking, agreeing to play hooky with Rosanna? It was that stupid glow she had from last night with Johnnie.

Sure, nothing had happened, they just hung out and got sodas, but it all felt so right, so clickety-click, that maybe she'd started to kid herself that there was something more there...

But that's all it was – kidding herself. This was a movie; there was a script and in this script, Johnnie was still in love with Rosanna.

She had to get a grip and stop acting as though this fantasy might be some kind of reality. On the other hand, there was a smell coming from the kitchen that seemed so real it could not be ignored.

The smell of pancakes, fresh off the griddle.

She popped her head around the kitchen door and her 'Mom' pulled her into the room and folded her in a warm embrace. It might not be real, but it felt soooo good.

As she looked up, her mom brushed a little tendril of hair from her forehead, kissed the spot where it had rested and then let her go and shooed her to the table, where a giant stack of fresh pancakes appeared in front of her.

This morning though, there was a new face at the breakfast table. The little brother, what was his name? Something weird: Badger? Haimster? Scooter? That was it, Scooter.

Looking at the mini mad scientist, buried behind a large text booked entitled *Building Giant Lasers*, she had an idea.

She tapped her finger on the table to get his attention. "Hey, Scooter!" He didn't even flicker.

"Scooter." Still nothing. "Scooter!"

She flipped the book down on the table with a bang.

Scooter jumped, then fixed her with an evil squint. "You'll be first." He picked up his book to start reading again, but Julie reached out and pressed it back onto the table.

"Yeah Scooter, that's nice, but I need to know – do you know anything about time travel? Bending reality dimensions?"

Scooter looked at her, considering. His eyes narrowed. "Where's my real sister and what have you done with her?"

What the hell, Julie thought, and took a deep breath. "I'll take a bet we both know 'real' is a relative term here. Are you going to help me?"

There was a long pause. As their eyes locked, she could almost hear the cogs whirring as Scooter's mathematical brain weighed up the possibilities. Finally he spoke. "I don't offer aid to bodysnatchers."

Julie willed herself not to scream – she had a feeling this kid was the only person who might be able to help. One more try: "Could be an interesting experiment?"

Scooter eyed her and she could see she'd aroused his

curiosity. She bit her lip and held back from pushing him any further, she'd just got to hold on, hold on...

"It's so nice to see you kids talking for once. What's got you two so interested?" Mom placed a fresh pot of coffee on the table and Scooter poured an enormous cup, adding no sugar or cream and raised it to his lips without once breaking eye contact.

Mom waited, sensing something wrong. "Well?"

"Nothing!" they said simultaneously, but inwardly Julie cursed, knowing the moment was lost.

* * *

Rosanna heard the knock on the front door and – still eating the toast she'd secreted up to her room - ran down the stairs to answer, but Mr. Peterson was faster – damn! She huddled down on the stairs, peering through the banisters to see if it was definitely who she thought it was.

It was! Andrew was standing on the doorstep and she could tell from the back of Mr. Peterson's head that he was not impressed. Could the back of a man's head frown?

As Andrew opened his mouth to speak, Rosanna figured she'd better go rescue him.

She ran down the stairs, kissing her dad on the cheek as she bundled Andrew off the doorstep. "Great pate, Dad, but I gotta motor. Andrew's gonna walk me to school."

"Didn't you seem him just last night?" Yup, he was frowning from the front too.

"Hi, Mr. Peterson," Andrew ventured and stuck his hand out to shake.

Mr. Peterson didn't even look his way. He raised his eyebrows at Rosanna, who was fidgeting from one foot to the other, desperate to get away. "Can't stop, Dad, gonna be late for homeroom."

She grabbed Andrew by the arm, who gave Mr. Peterson a sheepish smile as he let himself be dragged off.

Rosanna didn't stop running until they rounded the tall, neatly trimmed hedge that cut off the lawn from the street (and her from her dad's view), only to be brought up short as a bicycle wheel screeched to a halt inches from their feet.

Looking up, Rosanna saw Johnnie, his usual smile in place, but an antsy feel washing off him. "Hey Rosanna, walk you to school?"

She felt Andrew squeeze her hand and turning to him, their eyes locked in a secret smile. She'd forgotten the best part of being a teenager – doing what you shouldn't. It was delicious.

Hearing a faint coughing, she looked back and realized Johnnie was still there. Why did he look so unhappy? Vaguely something Julie had said the day before drifted back to her: "Johnnie's been in love with you, just, forever."

This movie just got better and better.

Not that she was interested in Johnnie – not her type at all, too sensitive – but it had been a long time since she'd had an admirer in her life, overflowing with the old unrequited and giving her ego a regular boost. This was definitely another thing she'd missed about being a teenager.

"Hey Johnnie," she gave him a slow come-on smile.

"We're taking a day off. You should come with."

"A day off?" Johnnie did not look impressed.

Andrew interjected, "Sure, everybody needs a day off now and then."

Johnnie snapped a look at Andrew, but didn't answer him, all his attention immediately back to Rosanna. "You? You, Rosanna, are cutting class? You never cut class. I cut class. You don't cut class. And for *him*? I mean, this guy?"

Totally ignoring Johnnie's rudeness - God, this guy was so cool - Andrew looked at Rosanna with a disbelieving smile.; "You never cut class before?"

"Um, no. You have?" Rosanna felt her own cool halo waver.

"Yeah, all the time."

"Is that why you got kicked out of school?" She had to ask, but before Andrew could answer, Johnnie spoke.

"Hey, how about we get back to how you *are* gonna get kicked out of school."

* * *

Arriving around the corner, Julie heard Johnnie's last sentence and froze. Were they in trouble? She ran over to join the tense little group. "Who's getting kicked out of school? Did we get busted already?"

Confused, she could see Johnnie staring at Andrew with utter hostility, Andrew feigning indifference, and Rosanna?

Well, it was weird, but Rosanna seemed over the moon. Why would she be pleased that Johnnie and Andrew were fighting?

Just as it started to make sense, Johnnie turned to see

Julie and suddenly his body language changed. His face lit up with a dangerous smile.

"Julie! Principessa. Guess what? We're taking the day off!"

"Oh yeah, that." This was all getting totally confusing and Julie felt like she needed to get things back on track.

She turned to Rosanna and attempted to give what she hoped was a meaningful stare. "Look, Rosanna, I don't know, shouldn't we try to stay out of trouble? At least till the end of the week?"

She widened her eyes and waggled her eyebrows until both boys were looking at her strangely, but Rosanna affected not to notice. "It'll be fine, Jules. I'll get you to the Prom on time, don't worry."

Julie looked daggers at Rosanna, but then was distracted as Johnnie took her arm, pulling her close to him, his voice like honey. "Rosanna's right, this'll be fun. Kinda like a double date. Can't be a good girl all your life, can you?"

His body was leaning into her, but he was watching Rosanna from the corner of his eye, trying to gauge her reaction.

Julie felt rage well up inside her. It was too much to be thrown into this crazy fantasy with her all-time ideal guy in front of her, only to have him try to use her to make Rosanna jealous.

"Hey!" The tone of her voice was soft but threaded with steel and now she had Johnnie's full attention. She held his gaze. "Don't flirt unless you mean it."

For a long moment, Johnnie looked at her as though he'd never seen her before, but he liked what he saw.

Not breaking eye contact, he hooked one arm through Julie's and – with his free hand wheeling his bicycle – started to walk her down the street.

Glancing behind her, Julie saw Rosanna watching them go. She didn't look happy but right then, Julie was too thrilled to wonder much about how anyone else was feeling.

* * *

Julie had been right – Rosanna was not happy.

Why, she couldn't figure. She closed her eyes against the warm sun, Andrew's arms wrapped around her as they leaned out over the top rail of the *Lake Michigan Tours* boat.

Opening her eyes again, she saw Julie leaning over the rail next to her. And next to Julie was Johnnie, his back to the Chicago skyline, turning now and then to point out particular landmarks, but more often than not with his eyes on Julie's face, ignoring the magnificent view behind him.

Breaking off from her muddled thoughts, Rosanna tuned into Johnnie's murmured commentary.

"See, there's the Playboy building. Now that you're officially a dropout, you might have to go ask about a job."

Julie hit him playfully on the arm. "Shut up," she breathed, but she was smiling shyly. Johnnie moved closer into her and dropped his voice further till Rosanna couldn't hear him anymore.

She pulled Andrew's arms tighter around her waist and looked to where he was pointing at the Sears Tower in the distance.

What was this she was feeling? Well really, deep down,

Rosanna knew exactly what the problem was - she just didn't want to admit it, even to herself. But if she were to be honest, she would have to say she was jealous.

Not that she wanted Johnnie for herself, but Geez. Was it too much to ask that she could be the star of her own movie for more than five minutes?

Anyhow, Julie had made it crystal clear she wasn't interested in Johnnie. For reasons she alone knew, Julie was still hung up on her jerk of a husband.

It had been one of the fundamental tenets of their friendship, a big reason why they'd never fallen out in all these years – they didn't go for the same guys and the same guys didn't go for them.

That said, all the guys they'd dated/married/avoided over the years had had one thing in common – they were all jerks.

But Rosanna liked handsome, exciting jerks and Julie liked boring, controlling jerks.

That was another reason she knew Julie wasn't seriously into this guy. He might not be sexy or exciting, but you could tell he was a really, deep down nice guy. And Julie never went for nice guys.

So why couldn't she let Rosanna be the center of attention just this once?

"Hey, daydream believer, this is nearly our stop." She realized Andrew was talking to her. "Sorry?" She squashed the shameful, childish feelings deep down inside her and hoped they'd go away if she ignored them.

Johnnie was lit up from the inside, holding onto Julie's hand. "We thought we might go up Sears Tower."

"Yeah," Julie looked equally excited, "I've never been."

"Seriously?" Andrew turned to Julie, incredulous. "You're from Chicago and you've never been up Sears Tower?"

"Well, it's not like I've always lived here." Julie was oblivious as Johnnie too turned to her in disbelief.

"Yes. Yes, you have. Julie, we've been friends since kindergarten."

The penny dropped. Julie stared at Rosanna, frozen in panic, but what could she do to help? Rosanna watched in horror as Julie started to babble.

"I mean, I mean, you know..." The air seemed to thicken around them as she groped for an answer. "Well, you know what I mean, I mean I haven't lived in the city. I'm from the burbs... I'm a burb girl, yeah..."

Julie trailed off, fake-laughing, a look in her eye like one of those racehorses you see that's about to get shot in the head. She looked desperately to Rosanna for a reprieve.

"But why would you say...?" Andrew started to speak but Rosanna - finally seeing a distraction - cut him off, pointing to the distance. "Is that a parade?"

Following her direction, the boys squinted to where the Von Steuben Day parade – Chicago's annual celebration of all things German-American - was indeed rolling through the streets.

Perched atop a float full of lederhosen and dirndl clad lovelies was a tiny, dark-haired figure. Music floated out across the water – he seemed to be singing *Twist and Shout*...

Behind the boys, Rosanna caught Julie's eye and they both breathed out.

9

This early on a weekday morning, the Sears Tower observation deck was quiet and calm.

Standing on the lower guard rail that ran around the deck, Rosanna, Johnnie and Julie leaned forward, their foreheads pressed against the glass.

Looking down at the tiny cars and people below, it felt as though they were floating above the city.

"It's so peaceful up here," Rosanna breathed, and they all paused in silence, feeling the truth of what she'd said.

Remembering something, Julie looked up. "Hey, you know you can see four states from here." She started to point them out, "There's Illinois, Michigan, Wisconsin and that's Indiana."

Johnnie looked at her in undisguised pride and admiration. "I thought you said you'd never been here before – how come you know all this stuff?"

Rosanna saw Julie blush. "Oh, I learned everything I know from the movies."

God, thought Rosanna, would Andrew ever get back from the bathroom? She felt a total gooseberry here.

Seeing Julie and Johnnie glowing inside their little bubble of new flirtation, Rosanna felt jealousy like bile rising up in her again and she couldn't seem to stop it belching out, "Yep, that's our Julie – always alone with the VCR on date night."

Julie blenched, obviously hurt, but Rosanna could barely even see her, she felt so consumed by her resentment.

She slid closer along the bar to Johnnie till their forearms touched, forcing his attention onto her, and dipped her head down to his, speaking softly. "So Johnnie, how come you never asked me to cut class with you before? We could have been stuck in detention together for hours."

She dropped her voice further, so he had to lean in even closer to hear her and pouted her lips around the *oooww* sound, drawing it out almost to a moan. "Hours and hours."

Bingo! She could practically hear a cartoon *twang* in Johnnie's pants as he cleared his throat nervously. "Oh, well, uh, it doesn't take hours." She held his gaze and bit her thumb as he continued to stutter his reply. "Um, detention, I mean, it's really not as bad as it's made out. I've made some very lasting friendships on a Saturday morning. Ha, yeah..."

He trailed off into silence.

Yes! thought Rosanna, ignoring Julie's stony face behind Johnnie, I've still got it.

Andrew appeared, and Johnnie finally broke his gaze away from Rosanna, shaking his head as if waking from a dream. "Oh, you're back? Good, great, I've needed the john for, like, the last half an hour. Gotta go!" And looking strangely relieved, he jumped down from the rail to go.

"But..." Julie sounded confused. "If you both needed to go, why didn't you just go together?"

Now it was the boys turn to look confused. Johnnie was the first to respond. "Julie, we're guys." Happy in the knowledge that he'd provided an obvious and logical explanation, Johnnie left for the men's room.

Maybe it was being in an alternate reality, maybe she was still distracted by Johnnie and Rosanna, but Julie still didn't look like she was getting it. Andrew took her hand in mock seriousness. "We do not go to the can together. It's the guy code."

Julie and Rosanna looked at each other and rolled their eyes - of course, how stupid. Then Rosanna saw Julie's gaze harden. Uh oh...

"We got to go together right now, don't we Rosanna? To the bathroom."

Something told Rosanna this wasn't going to be time to do each other's hair and swap lipsticks. "I don't have to go to the bathroom."

"Well I do, and you're coming with me." Julie gripped Rosanna's hand and walked her across the deck in a manner that brooked no argument. As an afterthought, she turned back to Andrew. "It's the girl code."

Left alone on the observation deck, Andrew lifted one arm high above his head and sniffed his armpit. "Do I offend?" he wondered aloud to no one in particular.

***

Rosanna wasn't wrong – Julie *was* mad. Mad as hell. Watching the back of her stupid, attention-seeking head as they walked towards the bathrooms, she grabbed Rosanna and bundled her into the gift shop.

Resisting the temptation to shove her up against the nearest display of *I Heart Chicago* teddy bears and put an elbow to her throat, like they did to those perps on TV, Julie spat it out, "What do you think you're doing?"

"What do you mean?"

Rosanna's wide-eyed attempt at innocence just made Julie boil over with rage. "What do you mean, what do I mean? You know exactly what I mean. I mean Johnnie. What are you doing with Johnnie? You don't want him, so why are you flirting with him?"

Rosanna shrugged, infuriatingly. "What can I say? I'm a slave to my character. Why do you care?"

There were a lot of things Julie could say but, unable to articulate (or admit to) any of them, her mouth shut, opened, then clamped shut again.

Seeing her advantage, Rosanna closed in.

"Julie, this is my movie, and in this movie Johnnie's in love with me. I'm the main character here, the main attraction for once in my goddam life and it's nice. Why can't you just let me enjoy it?"

"Because you're just using him. You're being a total bitch."

Even as the words came out of her mouth, Julie knew she was going too far now, but she just couldn't stop. "For once in your life? Rosanna 'me first' Peterson, are you kidding me? Why are you leading Johnnie on when you don't even want him?"

"And you do?" Seeing Rosanna's face open in sudden comprehension, Julie realized she'd given the game away. She started to back out of the gift shop. "We should find the john..."

"Oh, you do." Rosanna was mad now too and she wasn't going to let this go that easily. "Oh Julie, of course, I should have seen, he's just your type of loser." She laughed. "Typical Julie, every sob story and sad sack you see, you just got to have them."

"Johnnie's not a loser."

"No, it's okay Julie, she's right."

Julie felt the blood drain from her face as Johnnie stepped out from behind a rack of postcards, clutching a tacky Sears Tower snowglobe. How long had he been there? What had he heard?

"What kind of loser would be in love with the same girl for eight years when she doesn't even know he exists?" Johnnie thrust the snowglobe into Julie's hands.

"Here. I think I'd rather you have this now," He left her standing, open-mouthed in shame and confusion.

Feeling a sob welling up in the back of her throat that threatened to choke her, Julie shoved the snowglobe at Rosanna. "I don't need your second-hand gifts."

She pushed past her friend. "Enjoy your day off from reality, Rosanna. Remember, it's gonna end."

Tears blurring her vision, Julie turned and ran from the shop.

***

Stumbling through the unfamiliar city, trying to work out how to find the bus home on her own, Julie tried to order her thoughts.

Why was she so mad at Rosanna? Sure, she was a selfish pain in the ass, but that wasn't exactly new, so what had made her lose it the way she did?

And where did Rosanna get off, accusing her of wanting Johnnie for herself? It was ridiculous. Crazy.

Inconceivable.

Even if she did want Johnnie – and that's not to say that she did – it was just stupid to even think about it. All they had to do was stick to the script for a couple more days, and she'd be out of this nutso fantasy and back home, where everything made sense.

Back home, back to reality, back to Roger.

In spite of herself, Julie felt her heart sink.

She willed it to rise back up, trying to think of how great it would be to be home with Roger, but the only thoughts that came to mind were of Roger telling her she'd look great when she started going to the gym again while he scratched his own growing belly; Roger whining about her forgetting his favorite beer at the supermarket and accusing her of doing it on purpose.

Roger changing the subject when she tried to talk to him - again - about having a baby.

Now her heart wasn't just sinking, it was leaking, drowning in sorrow and grief for all the little babies she'd dreamed of and that Roger had promised her a long time ago.

A little voice at the back of her mind whispered that he'd stolen this from her, her dream of a family and that it was too late to get it back, but she couldn't think that way. She would never make it back to the surface.

Seeing her bus rounding the corner, she pushed the insistent voices deep down inside and started to run the last few yards to her stop.

* * *

Walking back out onto the observation deck and seeing Andrew leaning out over the city, Rosanna felt her gloom lift a little. She might have really messed up, but at least someone still loved her, even if he was fictional.

She crossed over and snuggled up under Andrew's

arm, keen for some physical reassurance.

He didn't disappoint, turning and kissing her gently on the forehead. "Hey, where're the others?"

She tucked herself in further, avoiding his gaze. "Oh, they decided to head off on their own, leave us to it."

"Cool." Andrew looked down and caught her downcast face before she could turn away. "Is that cool?"

"Yeah, sure."

Rosanna didn't know why but she felt... *ashamed*.

That was it, ashamed. She'd thought she was such a sex kitten, flirting with Johnnie, feeling her power over him. If she'd only known that Julie really liked him that much, she'd never have gone near him.

But goddam it, why did Julie have to be such a Miss Goody-Goody all the time? 'Oh no, I'm not even a little bitty-bit interested in Johnnie; I'm so in love with Roger the Wonder-Bore'.

Even here, on Planet Bananas, she couldn't admit for one second that her life wasn't perfect, just a big old mess like everyone else's.

And then when Julie had called her a bitch, she just saw red. Still, maybe she shouldn't have been quite so nasty. Shame started to creep through her again...

"What do you think?" Cutting across her thoughts, she realized Andrew was talking to her.

"What?"

"Where do we go next? I'm thinking the Institute of Art. What do you think?"

"Oh sure." Anywhere, thought Rosanna. Anywhere I don't have to think about what a bitch I've been.

* * *

Perfect, thought Rosanna.

Completely zoned out, she stood in front of Seurat's *A Sunday Afternoon on the Island of La Grande Jatte*. This had always been one of her favorite paintings and standing in front of the original now, close enough for the impressionist painting to fill her entire field of vision, was a totally zen experience.

Focusing on the wide open mouth of the little boy at the center of the idyllic picnic scene, she felt her mind clear and her heart rate drop to a steady pulse.

This was what she'd always loved about art – its power to transport her to a completely different emotional plane. No matter what else was going on in her life, she could go to a gallery and choose what to experience – great passion; melancholy; joy; wistfulness.

"You okay? You look a little sad."

Her train of thought broken, she looked up to see Andrew smiling at her and basked in his warmth and regard.

Could he be real? What if this was real life and the rest was the dream, would that be so bad? But then, life didn't seem to be working out that much simpler here. She sighed.

"You know, I always used to think life would be better if it were more like a movie. You ever wish that, that you could just step into your favorite movie and everything would be better? All the love stories would have happy endings, and everyone would learn an important life lesson and become a better person."

Andrew smiled at her wryly. "Your favorite movie's not gonna be a Bergman film, is it?"

She laughed. "No, it's Cannibal Holocaust."

The laugh still on her lips, she felt Andrew draw her close and turned her face in for his kiss. It was warm and sweet and felt oh so real.

Breaking off, she looked up to see Andrew's eyes dark with amusement and desire. "Can a movie do this for you."

"You'd be surprised." The irony made her a little blue again.

Turning away from his kiss, she took his hand and led him down the gallery, changing the subject as her eyes fell on more and more of her favorite artists.

"I used to want to be an artist," she blurted out. "A painter. Well, paint and collage. I wanted to make these huge pieces that would just envelop you and make you lose yourself, like a Stella or a Rosenquist."

This was leading her down another path she probably didn't want to go down. Shaking herself, she laughed it off. "Yeah, well, that was a long time ago."

"What happened? You make a big breakthrough in potato print and then, nada?"

Reddening, Rosanna realized her mistake. "Oh, well, I say a long time ago... Yeah, I guess, it just seems like another life."

"So why'd you stop?"

Rosanna paused, uncertain what to say without giving too much away. What could she say? That she'd had a kid, lost a husband and put her artistic ambitions on a permanent back-burner?

Vague, that was it. She'd settle for vague.

"Oh, I hardly even remember. I guess other things just got in the way."

"What's more important than doing what you love?"

And then she really saw him standing there, in all his wide-eyed innocence. Oh the hope and trustfulness of youth, that faith that if you worked hard and believed, everything would just magically work out how you wanted.

It made her want to slap him.

"You don't get it Andrew. There's more than one thing to love in life. God, you're so young."

"And you're too young to be so damn old." His words stung her like an icy wave. "You got to do it, Rosanna. You only get one chance."

"You would think, wouldn't you?" Time to change the subject, thought Rosanna, before this conversation led her astray entirely. "What about you? You can do anything you want, anything at all. What is it?"

Andrew's face lit up like a firework. "I'm doing it! Straight after graduation, I'm hitting the road, Kerouac-style." He turned to her, excited.

"You should come with!"

"Maybe I should."

Sure, what's the harm, thought Rosanna. She could entertain this fantasy a little longer. Everything was so great here, where was the harm in letting herself imagine it could last forever?

10

Finally, FINALLY, many hours later, after getting on the wrong bus twice and avoiding proposals of marriage from at least three winos, Julie clambered in her bedroom window and fell to the floor with a crash.

Shit! She heard footsteps on the stairs.

Reaching up, she quickly turned off the tape recording of noisy snores that was running on a loop, dragged a shop dummy from under the bedcovers, and slipped into the bed just in time as the door creaked open and Julie's mom poked her head around the door.

Struggling to regulate her breathing, Julie 'woke up' and lifted her head from the pillow. "Oh, hi Mom."

"Are you alright, Julie? I thought I heard a bang."

"Not me, Mom." Julie kept her face half under the covers to hide her burning cheeks. "Maybe Scooter left something running in his room."

Relief crossed her Mom's face. "Oh, you're probably right. I'll just go check."

Julie watched carefully as her Mom started to leave the room, tensing as she hesitated and turned back.

"How are you feeling now, honey? Your eyes are very red."

"Oh." What should she say? Julie wasn't used to anyone noticing that kind of thing – not when it came to her. "Well, I'm okay, I guess. I feel a little better."

"You want me to bring you up a hot chocolate?" Now here was something else Julie wasn't used to - maybe this vacation in Bizarro-land didn't have to be all bad.

"Really? Yeah, Mom, that'd be nice."

As she left the room, Julie threw off the covers and started to kick off her black pixie-boots and wrestle simultaneously with her black-suede fringed jacket.

CLICK! Quick as a flash, she whipped the covers up to her chin as the door crept open again.

"You want those little marshmallows on that?"

"Sure Mom, great."

The door closed again and Julie exhaled in relief, collapsing further into the cozy bed that smelled of fabric softener and home.

* * *

It had been a pretty successful day off for Rosanna. In spite of her falling out with Julie (and she was pretty sure she could talk Julie around – she always did), she had had an amazing day with Andrew and really, this fantasy world was starting to shape up pretty good.

As she sailed in the kitchen door of her new home, feeling pretty pleased with herself, she was brought up short by a stony-faced Mr.. Peterson.

"Where have you been today, Rosanna?"

She breezed past him and started to rummage in the cookie jar. God, she was hungry. Stuffing a cookie in her mouth, she answered through the crumbs. "Well, school, like always."

She carried on looking for unbroken cookies, oblivious to the unimpressed face of Mr.. Peterson behind her.

"Let's try again. Where have you been today, Rosanna?"

Uh-oh. She turned from the cookie jar and looked at

her 'father'. To say he did not look pleased would be the understatement of the century (the *twentieth* century, obviously).

She decided to play for time, "What's going on?"

"I had a call from the school. They wanted to know why you weren't in class today. So I'm going to ask you one more time. Where have you been today?"

Shit. Unable to think of a glib excuse, Rosanna tried the silent approach. How could she possibly be in trouble for skipping school? She graduated twenty fricking years ago!

"It's that boy's fault, isn't it?"

"Dad, no, this is not Andrew's fault."

"But he was with you today, wasn't he? I've been speaking to a couple of people about this Andrew. Has he told you why he got kicked out of his last school?"

Good point – did Mr.. Peterson have some juicy information? She'd love to know what the story really was there. "Well, no, but—"

"He didn't even tell you that? Well if he doesn't have that much respect for you, I'm not going to tell you, young lady. Now get up to your room and you'll be lucky if I let you out again before Thanksgiving."

Rosanna had to smile; it was so beyond ridiculous. "I'm grounded? Seriously? Wow, blast from the past."

Her amusement shrank as Mr.. Peterson shoved his angry face right up to hers and dropped his voice to a growl – where was the nice guy who wanted to be his daughter's best friend? "You live under my roof? You want my money to go to art school? You will do exactly what I say."

Then, just as abruptly, he turned away and started

washing cups at the sink.

Uncertain, Rosanna stared for a while at his hunched shoulders, waiting for the sweet, kind, indulgent daddy to reappear, but it looked like he'd left the building, least for now anyways.

For lack of a better option, Rosanna climbed the stairs and shut herself in the pink bedroom.

* * *

Snuggled under a cozy plaid rug next to her mom, Julie reached into the bowl in front of her for another handful of fresh, buttery popcorn. The salty corn together with the creamily-sweet hot chocolate was such a perfect combination, why had she never thought of this herself?

The movie lovers on the old black and white romance unfolding on the TV kissed passionately, and Julie and her mom sighed as one.

"This is nice," Julie murmured, "Do we do this often?"

"I guess." Her mom turned to her as she reached for the popcorn. "You think we do this too much?"

"No." Better not say any more, thought Julie. This was one part of this experience that was better than the real thing. Iona Placid was the mom she'd always dreamed of having when she was a kid.

She shouldn't get too used to this.

"Honey, can I ask you something?"

Uh oh, thought Julie, she knew this moment had to be too good to last. She took another handful of popcorn and kept her eyes on the TV screen. "Sure Mom, ask away."

"Julie, were, uh, were you honestly sick today?"

Julie paused, the popcorn almost at her lips, unable to meet her mom's eye.

"Well, yeah Mom, you know I was sick. I know I didn't have a temperature, but I had real bad stomach cramps and I had clammy hands, remember?"

Finally turning to her mom and making her best effort to look at her directly without giving herself away, she held her hands up. "Clammy hands?"

Unable to keep it up any longer, she dropped her head and snuggled up to her mom, hiding her reddening cheeks.

Iona stroked her hair gently. "I know. I just wondered if there was anyone you were trying to avoid today, like maybe a boy?"

Julie drew her head in like a turtle, as if it was possible to hide any further and nibbled nervously on a piece of popcorn.

Realizing she wasn't going to get an answer, Iona gently persisted.

"I'm just asking sweetheart because you seem different these past few days. And I don't think those red eyes are from stomach cramps, are they?"

Still Julie couldn't answer. She was fighting too hard not to start crying like a baby.

"You know you can tell me anything, Julie? You're my little girl and I love you."

That was it. It was all too much, and Julie just couldn't hold out against this tide of unaccustomed kindness and affection.

With tears escaping from her eyes, Julie finally lifted her head and met her mom's gaze. "There is kind of a boy."

She closed her eyes and winced, waiting for the punchline. This was the point where her real mom would have turned the tables, victorious that she'd gotten the truth out of Julie, gleeful that she'd found a weakness that she could use any time Julie tried to stand up to her about her drinking, about her violence, about anything at all. Here was something she could use to tease Julie unmercifully in front of her disgusting drinking buddies.

Julie tightened her eyes and waited for the drop.

But it didn't come.

"Do you think he's worth all this?" Julie opened her eyes and looked up. Iona was still looking down at her with love and concern, just like all those moms in storybooks.

Julie breathed out and found she couldn't stop; everything she'd been holding in just flooded out.

"Oh Mom, he's so worth it. He's just the sweetest, kindest guy. I liked him since I was a kid, but he's been in love with someone else for, like, a hundred years." Now the tears were coming and she couldn't stop them.

"And does she like him?"

"No!" As if, thought Julie. "No, it's so unfair, Mom, she doesn't even care about him and I do, and then I thought that maybe he might have noticed me but I guess no one ever does. I'm so stupid, I'm stupid..."

She was crying in earnest now and it was like every rotten thing that had ever happened to her in her whole rotten life was flooding out – all the stuff with her mom, every snide remark and not-so-subtle putdown from Roger, all the sneaky gropes and nasty threats to her job from Dirk. All the crap she'd put up with and glossed over for years and years and years washed over her, and at the same time, it felt so good to let it out, with Iona's arms around her making her feel safe and loved for the first time ever.

Through the haze of tears, she smelled fresh linen and was dimly aware of a soft, white handkerchief wiping her face clean. Iona shushed her as if she were a baby and pulled her in tighter for a hug. "You're not stupid. You're my clever, beautiful little girl and anyone who can't see that, well, he's, he's...he's just a shithead."

"Mom!" Julie was shocked out of her crying fit. Not that she was that prissy about cuss words, but to hear it from Iona?

Her mom looked a little flustered herself at what she'd just said. "Gosh, I'm sorry. I'm sure he's not, well, a doo-doo head if you like him this much. But you said you thought he'd noticed you?"

"Well, yeah." Julie sighed, resisting the temptation to sink back down into despair. "It seemed like that. But then the minute Ro—" She stopped herself. "This other girl so much as looks at him, he drops me like a hot rock."

"Sweetheart." Iona hugged her tight again, rocking Julie in her arms. "Oh, sweetheart, sweetheart. You really like this boy?"

Julie nodded, biting her lip.

"Well, go get him!"

Julie rocked back, shocked. Surely this was a little too much? But Iona was on fire now.

"You got to go tell him how you feel. This other girl," She waved her hand dismissively. "You say he's been in love with her forever, but she's giving him nothing back?"

"Well, yeah..." Where was Iona going with this? Different emotions – hope, fear, confusion – washed over Julie till she felt her brain might be facing the wrong way.

"That's not love, honey. That's a fantasy."

What isn't? thought Julie, but Iona wasn't finished. "He's just a young man with a lot of love to give and he needs someone to point him in the right direction."

Eyes shining with the conviction of a religious zealot, she stroked tendrils of hair tenderly from Julie's forehead. "Now, you clean up your face, put something pretty on and go tell him to stop wasting your time. What have you got to lose?"

"Uh, nothing, I guess." Swept away by Iona's faith in her, Julie felt hope rise up and win the battle for supremacy between her emotions, kicking fear to the curb and pushing pragmatism's head into the sand. Maybe Rosanna had been right all along. Maybe she could do anything she wanted here and be completely safe from consequences...

Seized with the possibilities, she flung her arms around her mom's neck and kissed her noisily on the cheek. "You're the best mom I ever had."

Iona blushed, pleased. "Go get changed, go on." She pushed Julie to her feet and shooed her out of the room.

Turning back to the black and white movie on TV, Iona sighed in satisfaction and a little regret – her little girl was all grown up.

If she only knew...

* * *

Trapped in pink hell, Rosanna flipped listlessly

through a magazine. It was hard to get excited about the details of Tom Cruise's fledgling romance with Mimi Rogers – her subject was art, not history.

Maybe Julie was right, she was dead already and destined to be grounded in this shrine to Pepto-Bismol for all eternity. She must have done something very, very bad.

A noise from the window distracted her.

She looked up as suddenly Andrew appeared through the window and slithered onto the floor, catching his head on the corner of the pink dresser.

She leaped from the bed. "Jesus, you scared me!"

Andrew scrambled up, rubbing a bump on the back of his head. "Couldn't wait to see you again. Whatcha doing?"

Rosanna slumped back down onto the bed and sighed theatrically. "Nothing. Like, officially nothing. For the rest of time, possibly."

Andrew looked at her quizzically.

"My Dad found out I cut school and I'm not even allowed out of my room. FYI, he blames you."

"Ouch! Guess I shouldn't stick around then." Andrew winced in mock pain, but he was grinning. Well, good for him, this was obviously *hilarious* fun from the outside. He wasn't the one who was stuck here with nothing but out-of-date gossip for company.

Rosanna tossed the magazine.

"Oh fuck it! This is ridiculous, He's all nicey-nicey, 'I'm your friend, not your dad', but it's all such bullshit. With my son—Or, I mean, daughter, like, if I ever have kids, I'm gonna actually be their friend."

"And you'll be like, 'Hey Son, I'm so glad you cut

school today. Let's blow off the whole semester together and go shoplifting.'"

Rosanna looked up and saw something in Andrew's eyes she definitely didn't like.

Was this, this man-child criticizing her parenting style? As if he knew anything. She drew her mouth into a sulky pout. "Quit ragging me."

"Well, stop being such a whiny brat!"

Her mouth fell open in shock. This was supposed to be her fantasy life – why was she getting such a hard time? Julie had been right – this was hell.

Andrew's face softened. "I didn't mean that. Well, I did, but I'm sorry. Look, after I got kicked out of school..."

Oh yeah, thought Rosanna, this was finally getting a bit interesting. "So why did you—"

Andrew cut her off firmly. *Damn.* "After I got kicked out of school, my parents were mad. I mean, I thought my dad was gonna bust a vein and die right there in front of me, but I knew they still loved me. I guess, really, that's how I knew they loved me."

Yeah, right, thought Rosanna. "Because they yelled at you?"

"Because they give a shit."

Whatever, thought Rosanna, then brought herself up short. God, being a teenager again was beginning to affect her mind as much as her body. All those crazy hormones were no easier to deal with the second time around. She looked up again at Andrew, considering.

"Do you think you'll ever have kids?"

"God, I hope so." Andrew smiled and, for a moment, Rosanna could see the man he was going to grow into –

passionate, kind, dependable. She'd never thought she'd see all those qualities together, but maybe she'd wasted a long time looking at the wrong men.

She felt sad for a moment, thinking how different it might have been to raise a son with a man like Andrew and jealous of the girl who would get to do just that.

Lost in her thoughts, she saw Andrew do a double take and laugh. "I mean, not right now!" He'd mistaken her silence for shock. "But sure, one day. And when I do, I want to be their Dad, you know? Maybe not exactly like my Dad, I want to do some stuff different. But I do want my kid to look at me like, 'Yeah, he's my Dad, he's the man', you know? Your Dad loves you."

Rosanna bristled again at Andrew's presumption. "Yeah, he loves me so much he threatened to pull my fees for art school."

"Double ouch. Why do you need to go to art school anyway, can't you just paint?"

Okay, so maybe Andrew wasn't all growed-up just yet. Ignoring his casual dismissal of her all-time, number one dream, Rosanna turned back to her thoughts about Gib.

"I'd just like to feel that, um, if I had a kid, they could tell me anything."

"Sounds great, you freakazoid." Andrew was laughing now, oblivious to Rosanna's rising anger. "What are you going to give your kids to rebel against?"

"Why do they need to rebel against me? Why can't we just be close?"

"Yeah, give me a call in twenty years and let me know how that's going for you." Andrew was on a comedy roll, with no idea of the giant nerve he'd just hit. "They'll either end up following you into the old folks home, wearing matching sweaters, or you're gonna end up the mom in Psycho, preserved for eternity by your loving son."

"I'd be a good mom." Rosanna's conviction wavered, her voice small, but Andrew was rolling around now, overcome by his own hilarity.

"Oh yeah, I can just see you now, looking after a kid." His voice became high and wavering. "'Mommy dearest, let's go to the movies together and then we can braid each other's hair!'"

"Shut the fuck up!" Rosanna aimed a cushion squarely at his head and – already off balance from laughing so hard - it knocked him off the edge of the bed and he hit the floor with a thump.

Within a millisecond, Mr.. Peterson's head appeared around the door. Rosanna instinctively looked around, but Andrew was hiding where he'd fallen, behind the frilly bed.

"Everything alright in here?" Mr. Peterson looked around suspiciously.

"Sure Daddio. A-okay." Rosanna picked up her magazine again and tried to look casual.

He wasn't buying it. Scanning the room to the left, then slowly to the right, he fixed his eye on Rosanna again and waited for her to crack. Rosanna felt her face strain with the effort to look innocent.

Finally, *finally*, Mr.. Peterson blinked first. Giving another quick sweep of the room to let Rosanna know that he wasn't completely buying it, he left, slamming the door.

Rosanna exhaled noisily, blowing out her cheeks in a

dramatic expression of relief, then turned to see Andrew's face, red with suppressed laughter, rising slowly over the edge of the bed.

Lifting her head, she tossed a teddy bear overhand and scored a direct hit to his face, then fell back on the pillows, spent with tension.

* * *

Quietly, Julie crept up the stairs to the studio apartment that Johnnie shared with his older brother. Except his brother (and legal guardian) was in jail, but the school authorities didn't know that yet.

Her hair was swept high off her neck and she had found a beautiful fifties-style prom dress in her wardrobe. In her nervousness, she felt the tickle of every tiny tendril of hair that escaped and brushed her neck.

The door was shut but, when she tried it, not locked. The sound of *The Smiths* playing on a cheap boombox drifted out as she pushed the door.

Peering in through the crack, she could see Johnnie sitting on a bare mattress, disconsolately flipping playing cards into an upturned hat. He hadn't noticed her. She could still slip away and he would never know the difference.

She took a deep breath and pushed the door open, tapping the floor lightly with the toe of her ballet flats.

Johnnie looked up and saw her there. His eyes clouded for a moment in confusion. She hesitated, smiled, and then his eyes cleared and he smiled right back at her.

The world stopped.

11

As the sun broke through the windows early next morning, Julie hesitated.

This wasn't her bed.

Then she remembered – of course, she was still in la-la land, in her perfect house with her ideal mom and dad, straight off of the back of the pancake packet.

She stretched, luxuriating in the relief of having two more days in dreamworld. She opened her eyes and watched dust motes dance in the shafts of sunlight that cut across the room.

Johnnie's room.

As she shifted, Johnnie turned in his sleep and snaked an arm around her. Oh God, they really were both naked. This was not good.

Even as her body lazily reveled in the sense memory of the previous night, her mind raced ahead. What had she done? Well, she knew exactly what she'd done, but how could she have got so caught up in the fantasy?

This was so, so, so wrong!

She had to get out of here. She started to sit up, but Johnnie woke and pulled her close to him. "Hey, Principessa."

She froze in his arms. "Oh God."

"Well, I can call you Principessa, you can call me God, if you like. Some women prefer Holy Savior..."

He trailed off, seeing Julie's look of horror and misinterpreting it. "I'm joking. I know you would think I have a lot of other women, but I promise there's only you."

As he slid from jokey nervousness into tenderness and kissed her softly, gently, Julie started to melt into his embrace. She was sliding down into the softest, sweetest oblivion and she never wanted to wake up.

Then she remembered and her body stiffened.

She had to be firm; she had to go now or she would never go. She pulled away, right out of the bed and started gathering her clothes. She had to get out of here now.

Turning, she saw Johnnie's confusion and felt her heart start to crack. No, she couldn't let herself even think about it. "Johnnie, we can't do this, this is wrong. It's so, so wrong."

He wasn't about to let her go easily. "What could be wrong?" He laughed that nervous little *ha* of a laugh, like he always did when he was upset. "I told you last night, I'm over that whole Rosanna thing, I'm an idiot. How could I ever have thought of anyone else?"

He moved towards her and reached for her hand. She drew back as if afraid, trying to ignore the hurt on his face, but unable to stop the guilt that was spreading over hers. She tried to turn away but it was too late, she saw the change in him as realization clicked into place.

He spoke slowly, "But there's someone else for you, is that it?"

"Oh Johnnie, it's complicated." Misery engulfed her as she saw his face harden against her. She should be glad – this was necessary. It could only be her vanity that wanted him to want her when she was determined to leave this room and never even think of him again.

She turned to leave, but Johnnie grabbed her wrist and yanked her back around to face him. "It's complicated? What does that even mean? It's real simple. Story of my life – I finally meet the perfect girl and she already has the perfect guy."

Faced with his anger and contempt, when he had been so gentle and so wonderful, Julie could barely croak out a reply. "I didn't say that."

"So he's not the perfect guy, just another scumwad with a great girlfriend. Hey, that sounds kind of familiar too!" His voice rising, he dropped her wrist and spun away from her.

Hot tears fell from Julie's eyes. "I'm sorry."

He wouldn't even look at her now. "Don't be sorry. Just tell me who he is. How do I not know this guy, does he go to our school?"

Oh God, how to begin to explain? "No. You don't know him." Julie stumbled over the words that felt like rocks in her swollen throat. "He's kind of...older. And he lives far away. I haven't even really spoken to him for a while."

Overwhelmed she sat down hard on the mattress on the floor and blew out her cheeks. "A really long while."

Seeing her utter defeat, Johnnie softened, sitting down next to her. "Julie, you're like, speaking a language I don't understand here."

He brushed a tendril of hair from her reddened eyes, and she glanced up, sheepishly, but couldn't reply. "You're with a guy, but I've never seen him. He lives far away and you don't speak anymore. I know that's the fairytale that every girl dreams of but..."

What could she say? "I know it doesn't sound great, but I made a promise."

Johnnie half-laughed. "Oh come on, Jules. It's not like you got married or anything."

Julie's stomach lurched. She stumbled back to her feet, grabbed her purse, almost blind in her panic. "I-I have to go. I have to get out of here. I'm sorry. I love you. I got to go."

Open-mouthed in shock, Johnnie watched her leave. Did she just say she loved him?

***

Rosanna was woken by strange little grunts and scuffling noises. Was there a groundhog trapped in the attic? Reluctantly opening her eyes, she was just in time to see Julie fall headfirst through the bedroom window.

She lifted herself up on her elbows and watched Julie struggle up from the floor. "God, doesn't anyone use the front door here? What the hell time is it?"

"Rosanna?" Something was wrong. Julie was stumbling, fighting with her skirts. She looked like she was about to burst into tears.

"Hey Ju, what's the matter?"

"We have to get home now."

"Ju, we've got like, two more days..."

"I can't wait for prom. I've got stuff to get back to... Roger— I've got a plan."

Rosanna paused, considering. What the hell?

"Fine, suits me. I got totally busted for skipping school and I'm not spending the rest of the week locked in here."

She drifted languidly out of bed and started to pick up clothes from here and there, finding one last outfit.

"Oh Geez, Rosanna." Julie was looking at her with disapproval, so at least *that* was back to normal. "You never cover your tracks."

Rosanna paused, mid lip-glossing. "This mean we're okay?"

Julie's eyes narrowed. "I didn't say that."

Damn, thought Rosanna, shouldn't have opened my mouth. Better change the subject again.

"So, what's your plan?"

* * *

Sneaking through the hall at Julie's house, they were nearly at the foot of the stairs when Iona appeared from the kitchen in a cloud of pancake fumes. "Julie, you weren't in your room this morning. The bed looked like it hadn't been slept in."

Seeing Julie lost for ideas, Rosanna stepped in front of her. "Totally my fault, Mrs. P. I was having a total wardrobe crisis this morning, so I called Julie and asked her over for breakfast."

Ha, thought Rosanna, never cover my tracks, do I? Well, now I've covered yours, so there.

Iona didn't look one hundred percent convinced, but she drifted back into the kitchen and Julie and Rosanna made their way upstairs.

Halfway across the landing, Julie stopped and motioned for Rosanna to get behind her. She crept towards a door with a large sign: DANGER: SCIENTIST AT WORK. KEEP OUT!

Smoke drifted out from beneath the door.

"Is that...? Should we...?" Julie just turned to Rosanna and put her finger to her lips, then inched forward towards the door and gently, *gently*, pushed it open a crack.

She waved Rosanna forward till they were both

looking in at a small, lab-coated figure hunched over a makeshift work bench. A welder's helmet shielded his eyes from the bright torch as he constructed what looked like a small nuclear warhead.

Rosanna's eyes widened, but Julie tugged her arm and directed her attention to the bank of computer monitors in the corner, green text scrolling on the black screens. "See that weird telephone set-up?"

Rosanna looked again. Next to the computers was an old-style telephone receiver resting on a dial-up modem.

Julie was hopping with excitement. "That's hooked up to NASA."

Rosanna didn't know what she'd expected, but she'd expected something better than this. "Great, brilliant plan. Let's call now and request a rocket back to reality."

"Oh Geez, Rosanna, use your imagination. Come on."

Really? But it was kind of nice to see bossy, take-charge Julie. Rosanna hadn't seen her in a long, long time. Not since...

But Julie was already barging her way into the bedroom. Rosanna skulked in behind her, but Scooter didn't even look up.

The girls hesitated. Julie attempted to break the silence. "Hey, what you doing, Scooter?"

Still no reaction. Julie tried again. "You got some big project you're working on there?"

They waited. Finally, Scooter spoke. "Since you know the rules about coming into my room, I'm going to assume that you're not really here."

Julie sighed, then caught Rosanna's eye and gave her a nod – time to put this plan into action. They sprang forward as one, lifting Scooter out of his chair as Rosanna swiftly disarmed him of the welding torch.

"Hey! You can't—" Julie clamped a hand over Scooter's mouth as they wrestled him to the floor. Julie held him as Rosanna unwound one of many scarves from around her waist and bound his wrists firmly.

"Sorry Scoots, but you were right. I'm not really your sister, I'm a visitor from another dimension so, you understand that I gotta do what I gotta do."

Scooter didn't look like he understood one bit. His eyes bulged with fury as Julie pressed a second scarf into his mouth.

***

Once Scooter was safely bound, gagged and stashed in his closet, Julie sat herself down in front of the banks of computers and started to work.

Hearing a muffled thump, Rosanna glanced nervously over her shoulder to the closet. "What if no-one finds him after we're gone? He's just a kid."

Julie continued to work, unfazed. "His mom'll find him."

Rosanna was still worried. "But all those notices on the door?"

"Oh please," Julie scoffed, "You see any dirty socks in here? Don't tell me his mom doesn't come in this room every day. I don't even have any kids. You're the one who should know this stuff."

Mollified, Rosanna turned back to see what Julie was doing. She looked again. Still not a clue. Did Julie have a clue? She hadn't even told Rosanna the whole of her amazing 'plan' yet.

"Do you have any idea what you're doing here?"

"I taught myself to code the store's website in HMTL5, I can do this 1980s shit." Finally looking up, Julie clocked Rosanna's skepticism. "Come on, it's a fictional computer – how hard can it be?"

Julie frantically typed more lines of code into the computer then suddenly stopped, reaching into her purse to pull something out – two white bras, one of which she thrust as Rosanna. "Here, put this on your head."

Rosanna looked down at the large, functional white bra in her hand, then looked back up at Julie, who was busy tying her bra around the top of her head, straps hooked under her chin so the cups stood up like the ears on Minnie Mouse. "You have completely lost your mind."

Julie looked at her as if she was the crazy one, then grabbed the bra from Rosanna's hands and started to tie it on her head.

"God Rosanna, didn't you ever pay any attention at the movies, or were you too busy necking in the back row." She ignored Rosanna's wince as she tied it tight under her chin. "It's ceremonial!"

Obviously, in her damaged mind, this all made perfect sense, but Julie had actually gone batshit crazy. Rosanna sighed inwardly. Might as well play along and wait for this nervous breakdown to burn itself out.

Out of the corner of her eye, she saw Scooter wriggle out of the closet door, still bound from head to foot and moving along the floor like a caterpillar. Never mind.

Julie was digging through her purse again, pulling out scarves, lipsticks, magazines...

"Aha!" She uncurled a copy of Scientific American with a picture of a black hole on the cover. "This is what we need; we need to make a black hole."

This was going too far. "Jules, wait, you're gonna kill us! Don't black holes crush people into teeny-tiny little pieces?" What if Julie actually managed to do... whatever it was that she was trying to do? Even Scooter looked worried, his eyes widening and his caterpillar crawl towards the door speeding up.

Julie was frantically clipping the electrodes that snaked out from one of the computers to either end of the magazine. "Just trust me. We're in a movie; this is movie logic. Now!"

She jammed the *ENTER* key on the keyboard and...

Nothing.

Rosanna breathed out. Thank God! Julie's nutty plan had come to nothing. She almost had Rosanna believing she could do it, for a minute.

Then slowly, slowly, a low rumbling crept through the house. Their computer chairs started to roll as the floor shook and the lights flickered.

There was a crash of thunder and Rosanna ran to the window and thrust the curtains aside to see the blue sky fill with black storm clouds, edged in red and ripped with lightning. She turned back to Julie in panic. "Shut it off. Shut it off now!"

"I'm trying!" Julie's finger was jammed on the power button of the main server, but the monitors continued to strobe with scrambled, incomprehensible text. She dove under the table and pulled the plug from the wall.

Still the computers stayed on!

The whole house was going crazy.

* * *

Down in the kitchen, Iona tried to gain control as pots boiled over on the stove, the popcorn popper sprayed in all directions, the blender spewed milkshake and something green and slimy exploded in the microwave.

* * *

Upstairs, Scooter spun round and round, the scarves that bound him trailing out in all directions as his feet lifted off the floor. Julie made a grab for him as he floated to the ceiling, but Rosanna pulled her back to their hiding place under the workbench.

* * *

In the den, Doug Placid was enjoying the morning paper and his first pipe of the day, oblivious to the flickering of the lights as the house shook around him. At last an almighty CRASH from right above his head forced him to look up.

"Hmph. Kids." Shaking out the paper, Doug returned to a very interesting article on the prospect of portable handheld televisions. *Handheld televisions*! Who would want to watch TV on a screen that small?

* * *

Back in Scooter's room, Julie and Rosanna frantically pulled leads out from every socket they could find to no avail. The dot matrix printer was spewing out reams of white and green striped paper.

In desperation, Rosanna picked up a baseball bat that was leaning by the window and swung it at the computer station. The bat shattered into a million pieces, like a rose dipped in liquid nitrogen.

Then suddenly all the noise – the chatter of the printer, the thunder, the wind screaming through the open window – ceased and the girls were plunged into total darkness.

Darkness and silence.

Her heart thumping against her ribcage, Rosanna reached out and found Julie's hand, squeezing it tightly. "Is this the vortex?"

"Shh!" Julie squeezed Rosanna's hand tight as a low hum pierced the velvet blackness, growing and growing until...

The ceiling light came on. They'd never left Scooter's room.

The girls let out a sigh, and then froze as they saw Scooter, apparently released from both the scarves and the constraints of gravity, standing on the bedroom ceiling.

He looked right back at them and nodded his head, a smile of nerd satisfaction spreading across his elfin face.

"Oh yeah, this is cool. You guys can stay."

Eyes locked on Scooter and clinging together from the sheer relief of being alive, neither Julie nor Rosanna noticed a small, whirling vortex open up underneath Scooter's computer table.

It spat out a black Betamax tape decorated with small, gold stars and, with a little sucking sound, disappeared again.

12

So, they might have travelled across time, space and reality, changed the course of (fictional) history and opened up a small black hole (even if they didn't know that yet), but apparently, they still had to go to school.

Julie and Rosanna stumbled down the pavement, dazed and disheveled, their smoke-blackened faces and hedge-backward hair-dos in stark contrast to the rows and rows of candy-colored houses and neatly clipped hedges that made up Julie's neighborhood.

Julie was the first to speak.

"I think I lost my virginity again."

"Oh." Rosanna struggled hard to comprehend what Julie was telling her, but her brain felt like it was in the spin wash.

And Julie hadn't finished yet. "I can't work out if it counts as cheating or not."

"I dunno, I mean, if you're not you..."

"But I *am* me, all the time. I mean am I? Aren't I?"

"Oh God, Ju, this is too existential. I'm gonna vomit."

Rosanna lurched towards a nearby hedge but righted herself just before she added some leaves to her birds-nest hair. Then something occurred to her. "So Julie, was it—?"

Julie cut her off, a glow spreading over her greenish face. "Oh Rosanna, it was beautiful, it was, you know..." She smiled shyly. "It was just like the movies."

"No, Julie, I meant was it Johnnie?"

"Oh!" From green, to glowing, to bright red, Julie

was a veritable kaleidoscope this morning. "Of course it was Johnnie, what do you think—?"

"Just checking." *Thank God*, thought Rosanna, this should get her off the hook for yesterday. Julie couldn't be mad at her for flirting with Johnnie when she got what she wanted. Or didn't want, it was hard to tell with Julie sometimes.

Looking up, Rosanna saw a little old lady walking towards them, a yapping Pomeranian on a leash. The old lady shrank back in horror at the sight of the two girls in tattered clothes and singed hair. Rosanna stuck her tongue out and the old biddy scurried away.

She turned back to Julie. "So what do we do now?"

"Well," Julie considered, "you have to go to school 'cause we're still *here*, which means you're still grounded."

Rosanna slapped her forehead and groaned aloud. She'd forgotten. "How can I be grounded? I'm thirty-eight years old!"

Julie looked at her sideways. "You were thirty-eight last year."

Smartass, thought Rosanna. "Yeah, well, I was eighteen this morning. What's the big diff?"

Julie smiled. "The big diff? You really are aging backward."

But she'd smiled. Rosanna had made her smile. Now was maybe the time to test the waters, see how the land lay, and throw out some other geological metaphors.

"Look, I'm sorry about...about yesterday."

Julie continued walking at Rosanna's side without looking towards her. "Good. You should be."

Okay, so the ice was broken, but they weren't

through the rocky patch yet. Then she saw Julie's eyes slide sideways towards her and a smile spread half across her face. Maybe they were on solid ground again.

BANG! Without warning, Julie shoulder charged Rosanna.

"Ow!" Rosanna rubbed her shoulder and looked balefully at Julie, who was grinning ear to ear. "You done now?"

"I'm done." And Julie walked off ahead, an extra spring in her step.

* * *

The school science lab buzzed faintly, a background hum to the boredom of twenty students in graying lab coats and plastic goggles. *Geez*, thought Julie, she'd forgotten how uncomfortable these goggles were.

She slid a finger under the thick plastic rim and scratched her nose.

As they shuffled behind the benches, waiting for the teacher to show, Rosanna poked speculatively at the little jars of gray gravel that sat in front of each pair of students. Ow! That gravel just bit her! She poked it again. "Ow!"

"Stop that!" Julie slapped her hand away.

"It hurts." Rosanna rubbed her sore fingertips together.

"Stop poking it then."

Any further tussle they might have had was cut short by the arrival of Doctor Maxine Jones.

Dr. Max's blonde curls stood around her head like the aftermath of an explosion (and could have been, given her reputation). Crackling with excitement and maybe something else, she strode to the bench that faced the front of the class and straightaway picked up a piece of the gray gravel with a long pair of tweezers.

Julie nudged Rosanna, "See?"

Rosanna rolled her eyes at Julie and mocked a large yawn as Dr. Max began to speak.

"Today, class, we're going to be looking at Lithium, a funny little element that I personally ingest every day, although I don't suggest you eat it raw like this."

Most of the class gazed at her in silence, a mixture of bemusement and the fact that a lot of them were still waking up for their first class of the morning.

But one kid raised his hand. *There's always one*, thought Rosanna...

"Ummm, why not?"

This was the question she'd been waiting for. In response, Dr. Max dropped the piece of Lithium from her tweezers into a bowl of water where it promptly burst into flame and whizzed, still burning, across the surface.

"Remember," said Dr. Max, a note of triumph in her voice, "your body is eighty percent water. So. No. Licking. The. Lithium. Now I want everyone to gather around."

Roused by the prospect of severe injury and/or flamey destruction the students flowed down to the front bench, for once eager to be at the front. "Not too close!" Dr. Max held up a hand, not noticing Julie and Rosanna loitering far behind the back of the crowd.

Eyes front, Rosanna tapped Julie on the forearm and whispered urgently: "Any other bright ideas to get us out of here? It is hell. I'm in high school for all eternity."

"Shhh!" Julie looked up, but Dr. Max and the rest of the class were fully engrossed in the hissing, multicolored results as the eccentric teacher added different chemicals to the lithium. "Tomorrow's the Prom. We just have to stick to the script for two more days."

"I guess so, but..." Rosanna looked to her left and trailed off. Julie had disappeared. Oh God, had her experiment with Scooter's computer that morning had a delayed effect?

Tap-tap-tap Now it made sense. At the window was the slightly more mundane reason for Julie's sudden disappearance: Johnnie was outside, trying to attract Rosanna's attention.

As she turned to the window, she felt a tug on her foot. Rosanna looked down and saw Julie under the bench, one hand wrapped around Rosanna's ankle, the other pressing one finger to her lips.

Shaking off Julie's hand, she shuffled towards the window.

Johnnie leaned close and whispered, "You seen Julie?"

"Errrrm, have I?" Rosanna felt a tug from under the bench. "No! No, I haven't seen her. Um, I heard she left town. Very suddenly."

Glancing down, Rosanna saw Julie's face fixed in a definite expression of *You cannot be serious*! Looking back up, Johnnie looked much the same. He opened his mouth to start questioning her, but Rosanna quickly cut across him.

"Oh no, that was me. Yes. I came back." Julie's head was in her hands, but officially she wasn't here, so Rosanna was just gonna ignore her. "She's sick. Yes, very sick. And contagious. Kind of swollen up and gross. Pustulous."

Johnnie did not look convinced. Well, tough. Julie could make up her own dumbass stories in future, or at least give her a five-minute warning.

She stared at Johnnie, brazening it out – she was damned if she was going to give him anything more.

Finally, finally, he cracked first. "Riiight. Well, if she makes a miraculous recovery, or comes back into town, tell her I'm looking for her. And tell her— Yeah, just tell her I'm looking, okay?"

"Will do!" Rosanna's cheeks ached in a ridiculous smile as she willed Johnnie to leave. This time she cracked first, turning to the bench to pretend to write up some lab notes until she was sure he was gone.

Out the side of her mouth she muttered, "You can't hide from him forever, you know?"

Julie's head bobbed up from beneath the bench. "I don't have to hide forever. I just need two more days."

"Right," Rosanna doodled on her 'lab notes'. "So you're going to go hide in a basement, and I've got to…?"

"Go home, break up with Andrew, go to Prom, have a fight, stick your hand in a VCR…"

"Okay!" Rosanna held up her hand against Julie's rising panic. "What about you?"

Julie looked doubtful for a moment. "I guess I'll just make sure I'm holding your hand when you get electrocuted."

Rosanna wasn't convinced. "I just hope this works better than your last plan."

"Well, that's how you got here. It'll work. It has to work this time."

"But what if it doesn't?"
Julie's face was set, furious. "It's going to work."

13

Well, we survived another day, thought Rosanna as she got off the school bus. She'd found her way home, Julie had managed to successfully avoid Johnnie for the rest of school and gravity hadn't been reversed since breakfast.

All in all, a success.

The early summer air was warm on her skin, the scent of leaves and fresh cut grass heavy in the air as she walked up the long driveway. She was definitely going to miss this vacation from reality.

As she reached the house, the garage door half-slid up and her dad ducked out from under it, dressed in paint- spattered coveralls and wiping his hands on a rag.

Judging from the amount of white paint in his hair too, he'd obviously been up to something. He smiled broadly at Rosanna.

"I've got a big surprise for you."

"Am I not still in trouble?" Not that she wanted to be, but hey, best to check.

Mr. Peterson looked uncomfortable for a moment, but shrugged it off. "No, well, I'm not saying that. But you got a bunch of letters today, and this one on top has an Art Institute of Chicago stamp."

He pulled a stack of mail from the large front pocket of his coveralls. Rosanna snatched them from his hands before he could offer them. What had Julie told her about a scholarship?

Shuffling through, she pulled out one letter with trembling hands. "This one is postmarked Paris."

She ripped it open, reading as fast as she could, and looked up at Mr. Peterson with shining eyes.

"The scholarship! It's true! Oh my God, it's true, I really got in!"

She flew at her fictional father to hug him, but he held her back, his arms stiff and smile frozen on his tight face.

"You didn't tell me you'd applied to Paris. It's a long way to go when you've got the Art Institute right here on your doorstep." His tone was deliberately genial, but Rosanna was so excited she missed the thread of ice in what he was saying.

She gazed down at the letter in her hands, reading and re-reading, and then reality began to sink in. "Paris. It's not gonna happen for me, is it?"

Thinking she was agreeing with him, the warmth returned to Mr. Peterson's smile. "You gotta be realistic, sweetheart. There's something else too."

Rosanna was lost in her own world, barely noticing as he lifted up the garage door with one hand and steered her by the elbow, with the other.

He was still talking. "I figured you'd need some space when school starts, somewhere to work on your own projects undisturbed."

As the garage door opened fully, Rosanna finally looked up – and gasped.

The inside of the garage was a blinding white, empty space, save for an artist's easel in the center of the floor. She walked into the space and turned and turned, overcome.

Mr. Peterson looked sheepish, still cleaning his hands on the rag. "Well, you won't get this in Paris. I'm gonna put some shelves up, maybe put a bench along this wall, but you got to let me know what you need for this to be a real artist's studio."

"Oh Dad," Rosanna breathed, "It's perfect. I don't know if I ever want to leave." And it was true. Not just having a space of her own to do nothing but create, but really, no one had ever done anything so kind and considerate for her before. It was the best present she had ever had.

Mr. Peterson brightened at her last words, his chest visibly swelling with pleasure and pride. "Rosanna, there are no second chances in life. That's why you're going to have to think seriously about your priorities."

"Priorities?" Rosanna still wasn't really listening, but a little warning bell sounded deep in the back of her mind.

Seeing her still preoccupied with her new studio, Mr Peterson took both her hands. "No one gets to have everything, sweetheart."

"What do you mean?" Rosanna should have known – there was always a catch.

"You're going to college; you're going places. This boy you've been seeing, you think he's headed in the same direction?"

"Oh, that!" Little did Mr. Peterson suspect, but for once they were on the same page, just for different reasons. "You think I should break up with him? Yeah, sure Dad, that's fine."

"Oh!" Mr. Peterson looked a little stunned. "Oh, okay, well…good. That's great honey, I'm glad we agr—"

"Yup," Rosanna cut him off before he could get suspicious. "Gonna break up with him tonight, that's the plan."

"Right, well, uh..." Poor Mr. Peterson, he wasn't prepared for this. "I'll, uh, I'll leave you to work out your new studio. You really like it?"

"I love it, Dad. It's the best. I wish I could stay here forever." She threw her arms around him in a ferocious hug then just as quickly let him go, turning back to survey her studio again.

Bemused, Mr. Peterson slipped away. He needed time to think.

* * *

Across town, Julie sidled in the kitchen door, praying she could make it to her room unnoticed. All she needed right now was five minutes of pure peace and quiet.

Not a chance. Sat right there at the kitchen table, drinking coffee were her mom... and Johnnie.

Damn.

She faked a natural smile. "Hey Johnnie, I didn't see your bike out front."

"You did check then." She took in Johnnie's stony face and her smile curdled.

Iona looked from Julie to Johnnie, sensing the tension, looking for a way to quell it.

She came across the kitchen and wrapped Julie in a hug, whispering to her as she did, "You didn't tell me he was so cute!" Then she stepped back and dropped the whisper. "I've invited Johnnie to stay to dinner, if that's okay?"

"Oh sure, Mom, great." Julie smiled queasily at her mother.

"Excellent. Looking forward to it, Mrs. P." Johnnie's eyes were on Julie, sparkling with aggression.

Iona knew all about a well-timed exit. "I'll just see if your brother's nearly ready if you kids want to set the table."

Alone, across the kitchen table, Julie couldn't think of one damn thing to say. Well, there was plenty she wanted to say, but nothing she was gonna.

Johnnie tapped his fingers on the table. "So, you look well. Not sick or, what was it, pustulous?"

Julie blushed and looked away.

"Are we gonna sit here in silence all night? You can't just blank me forever, Julie."

"Well...it's just... There's nothing I can say." Julie thought she couldn't sink any further into her misery.

She was wrong.

"Why don't you start with why you came over to my place last night? It's a pretty mean trick, Julie, to turn up like that, to stay. When you knew all along there was someone else."

Julie's deep shame was compounded by confusion. She'd done the dirty on Roger. So why did she feel like she'd cheated on Johnnie?

"I mean it, Julie." Johnnie wasn't giving up. "Why'd you come? Was it just to hurt me?"

"No!" Shock propelled Julie out of her silence.

"So why did you come?"

"Because I've always loved you," Julie shouted. Her hand flew to her mouth as if she could stuff the words back in.

A slow smile crept across Johnnie's face, but before Julie could blurt out anymore, in walked her mom, with

Mr. Placid's arm wrapped around her waist.

"Ohhhh," breathed Iona in mock surprise. "We're not interrupting anything, are we?" She giggled as Doug nudged her in the ribs.

Geez, thought Julie, who were the teenagers around here? Then again, these days, who knew?

***

Almost the whole family was gathered round the solid wood kitchen table – Iona, Doug, Scooter, Julie and - of course - Johnnie.

Ginny—blonde, beautiful Ginny—came flying through the kitchen, planting kisses as she went. "Bye Mom. Bye Dad." She turned a withering glance on her brother and sister, "Later, mutants."

Then the unexpected sight of Johnnie brought her up short. "Who are you?"

As Johnnie opened his mouth, Iona cut in, fizzing with excitement. "This is Julie's young man, Johnnie."

"Oh." For a moment, Ginny almost registered interest. She narrowed her eyes at Julie. "I thought you were a lesbian."

Then the moment was gone. "Whatever." She grabbed a piece of bread and bit through it as she breezed right out of the kitchen in a cloud of Babysoft and Wrigley's spearmint.

"Now." Iona started to fill plates with an incredible smelling casserole and pass them around. "This is real nice. Julie, Johnnie tells me he's taking you to Prom tomorrow night."

"Uh..." Julie looked up at Johnnie, mortified.

Johnnie leaped in first, "Yeah, if she'll still have me."

"Or if she's still here," Scooter muttered. Julie flushed red, and Johnnie turned, confused, but Iona wasn't listening – she was still distracted by what Johnnie had said.

"Why wouldn't she go with you? You guys haven't had a falling out, have you?"

Johnnie raised his eyebrows in a question, and Iona looked so crestfallen, Julie had to unfreeze her brain and start forming syllables. "No! No, everything's just fine, Mom."

She looked down at the plate of delicious casserole – would she ever get used to someone else looking after her? – and started to work her way determinedly through it, looking neither left nor right.

She glanced up and Johnnie was looking at her. He looked... *amused*. Julie didn't know right now if she wanted to kiss him or slap him. Probably slap him, right this minute.

Doug cleared his throat and decided to weigh in. "So young man, high school finishes soon. What do you intend to do with the rest of your life?"

"Dad, Geez!" Who knew fictional parents could be just as embarrassing as real ones? "Just jump in with the heavy questions already."

But Johnnie didn't look fazed. "No Julie, that's alright."

"Well, what do you like to do?" Julie didn't think she'd ever heard Doug say more than two words before – not here, and not when she'd watched this movie in reality. Then again, this scene never appeared in any movie.

This was getting really out of hand.

Johnnie looked a little thrown off now. "Uh, well, I like to play video games."

Everyone stopped in mid-air, or so it seemed to Julie. Then Scooter snorted, and Johnnie started to waffle.

"I actually, I programmed this game. It's for more than one player, remote, you know? On the TCP/IP Protocol Network."

Doug and Iona looked at him blankly. Scooter rolled his eyes with exaggerated despair. "He means the Internet."

Still nothing from Doug and Iona.

"Well, yeah, sure..." Johnnie looked really nervous now – was he sweating? "That's what the geeks call it." He reddened, seeing Scooter's face and knowing immediately he'd said the wrong thing again. "I mean, sorry."

He turned back to Doug. "Well, it's a text based game, but I think graphic games could go over the network soon, then you could have people from Japan playing kids in Europe, you could have multiple characters, build worlds..."

He trailed off, getting nothing back. Under the table, Julie kicked Scooter – the one person who might have been able to help Johnnie out – but he was obviously still sore at being called a geek and pretended not to notice.

Julie could practically see the tumbleweed blowing across the table. She had to help him out. "It could work. I think it's a great idea." And it was, but how could she convince Doug and Iona?

How could she possibly explain that in the future, this very idea would be huge business, that everyone would be on the internet (and at the same time, tell Scooter that one day, the name 'Geek' would be worn as a badge of pride)?

She trailed off, scared of saying too much.

Eventually, Doug broke the silence. "If you want, I could put in a word for you at the mill. We could do with some help computerizing our inventory."

"Um, yeah." Johnnie tried to look politely enthusiastic. "I guess what you really want to know is, am I gonna take care of your little girl?"

Scooter snorted again and started to cough into his napkin, failing to disguise his laughter. Julie kicked him, hard this time and he slid under the table.

Used to Scooter's eccentricities, Doug and Iona ignored him.

Johnnie barely even broke his stride. He was on his favorite subject now — Julie.

"I am. I am gonna take care of her. But, to be honest, I don't know what my specific plans are." He was still talking to Doug, but now his eyes were only on Julie. "I never really thought a lot about the future before. Now I look at Julie, and all I see is the future."

Iona melted visibly at Johnnie's words, but Doug seemed unconvinced. Looking back at him, Johnnie clocked Doug's stony face and faltered. "Uh, I guess I'm still working a few things out right now."

Another awkward silence.

Then Iona broke in, hesitantly, almost shyly. "'The future, stretching out beyond our dreams to the endless horizon.'"

As she spoke, Doug started to choke a little on his beer.

"That's beautiful, Mom. Who wrote that?"

Iona smiled a strange secret smile at Julie. "Your father did." She blushed with pride.

Julie swiveled around to face her father, shocked out of her discomfort. "I never knew you were a writer!"

"Hmph!" Doug Placid had never looked more uncomfortable. "I am not a writer. I sell cloth, yarns, and associated textile products. Wholesale."

He returned to his dinner with renewed vigor, but Iona wasn't done yet. "He is a writer. Your father was a beat poet."

"Far out, Mr. Placid!" Johnnie's attempt at humor faded as Doug turned a murderous glare upon him, but Iona knew and loved Doug too well to be put off.

"He used to write me beautiful poems and slip them into my books in class."

Julie was stunned. She'd been enjoying living with this fantasy family so much, it had never occurred to her that they had a life outside of their roles – their roles as her parents. She turned to her mother, "What about you, what did you want to be?"

Doug visibly relaxed – the spotlight was off and now it was Iona's turn. "Your mom was a wonderful singer. And she played guitar." He smiled at his wife, remembering.

Julie turned to her mother and raised her eyebrows. "Mom?"

Now it was Iona's turn to be embarrassed. "Oh, I was in this band. We were kind of like the B52's. Well, we thought we were, it was silly, really."

This dinner was just getting weirder and weirder. Somehow, to Julie, this was stranger even than waking up in a teenage body. Stranger than sleeping with the literal boy of her dreams Stranger even than attempting to open up a black hole between dimensions.

Her dream parents were turning out to be real people.

Johnnie had forgotten all the embarrassment of pitching his game ideas and was just enthralled by the unfolding revelations. "So what happened, Mrs. P?"

Iona locked eyes with Doug. "Well, you can't go on the road when you're knocked up."

"Mom!" Julie didn't think she could take much more of this.

Iona smiled gently at her. "Oh Julie, don't give me that goofy look. How old did you make out I was when Ginny was born?

Julie's mouth flapped like a fish out of water. "I just never thought..." I mean, she knew her parents had always looked young to have a twenty year old daughter, but she'd thought that was just casting.

Her mom cut straight across her: "And I hope you two kids are being more careful than we were."

"Mom, please!" Her surprise forgotten, Julie glanced across at Johnnie and saw written across his face the same guilt—and realization—that she felt at that moment. They hadn't been careful. They hadn't been careful at all.

Under the table she crossed her fingers and tapped the wood.

Iona was on a roll, relishing the shock on the kids' faces. "What can I say, I'm a modern woman."

"That you are." Doug gazed into his wife's eyes, remembering the love that started over twenty years ago.

Scooter pretended to retch over the side of the table.

"So," Johnnie leaped in, desperate to change the subject. "Mr. Placid, you still do any scribbling?"

"Well," Doug leaned back into his chair, stretching his arms out and cracking his knuckles in front of him as he settled in for a long talk. "They say a writer writes. And that's why I like to take the bus to work. You meet the real, raw people of America on the bus; every one with a story to tell…"

14

Later that night, Julie walked Johnnie to the end of her street, reluctant to let him go without some time alone. The evening was warm, and the air smelled rich and heavy with damp grass. Fireflies rose from the lawns lining the street, rising and extinguishing, falling again.

Julie was so distracted, she barely saw them. "It's like I opened up a door and found a room I never knew was there."

Johnnie smiled at her confusion. "What, you just thought your parents sprang into the world fully formed and said 'Hey, let's settle down and have a couple or so kids and I'll get a job at the mill'?"

How could she explain to Johnnie that that was exactly what she'd thought? "Well, kinda, yeah. They're like, real people. They have a whole life outside of, uh, this."

"Who knew?" Johnnie was teasing her now – but if *he* only knew…

He took her hand, and they walked on in silence for a while. Johnnie was content, contemplative, but beside him Julie's mind was a maelstrom.

If her parents had a past, one that she knew nothing about, one that was never mentioned in the movie, what did this mean?

If they could have a past, what did that mean for the future?

"The future?" Johnnie cut across her thoughts. Oh God, she'd already traveled across dimensions, reversed gravity and apparently brought fictional characters to life—could she now project her thoughts?

"Julie, are you listening? I meant what I said in there, about the future."

Relief flooded her body, and she blew the breath she'd been holding out with a sigh. "Oh Johnnie, what if the future never comes?"

"Oh, it's coming, Julie, whether you want it or not. Do you want it?"

"God, I don't know. This is hard." He had no idea how hard. This dream was getting to be just as complicated as real life, with every decision leading to consequences she'd never imagined. Wasn't this supposed to be a vacation from reality?

She turned to him, still holding his hand, and put out her other hand to stop him getting too close. "Why can't we pretend there's no tomorrow? Or, well, no day after tomorrow, anyway. No exams, no graduation. Tomorrow's the last day of your life – what do you want to do?"

In reply, he pulled her closer and kissed her gently, softly on the lips.

* * *

Meanwhile, Rosanna's thoughts were far from romance as she worked into the night in her new studio. How long had it been since she'd allowed herself this space, this freedom – this amount of time – to just create and play with new ideas?

As she stood in front of her canvas in baggy trousers and an old shirt of Mr. Peterson's, she was oblivious to the flecks of paint that spattered her face, her clothes, and her hair.

Suddenly, Andrew appeared in the open garage doorway: "Hey."

Rosanna jumped about a foot in the air, paintbrush clattering to the floor. "Shit, you've got to stop sneaking up on me—you scared me!"

"Well, I am a scary guy." Andrew strolled over, hands in pockets, to look at the canvas she was working on. "That's pretty good."

"Thanks." Rosanna blushed—a little from pleasure but mostly because this work was so far from ready to show to anyone. This was a sketch really, an idea in paint form and until it was more fully formed she felt as though she was exposing her insides; opening up her brain and letting people in with muddy shoes.

Andrew didn't notice her discomfort. He had his own agenda. "You should go to art school, you know. Somewhere like Paris, maybe?" He saw Rosanna's blush now and read his own meaning into it. "I saw your Dad He told me about the scholarship."

"He did?" Rosanna wasn't ready to start discussing this now. She had a story to stick to and that was all she needed to do right now. But how to explain?

She picked up her brush and turned back to the canvas, dabbing on tiny bits of paint, going over what was already done.

"He also said you're thinking of not taking it." Rosanna didn't look up, just studied the canvas even harder. But Andrew wasn't giving up.

"Are you nuts?"

This time Rosanna couldn't ignore him. She turned to him, furious, pointing her paintbrush at him to emphasize her words.

"Oh, grow up, Andrew. You don't get everything you want in life."

"Well, your dad seems to be getting everything he wants. You're just going to stay in Chicago, locked in this garage, playing happy family?"

"Is that what you think?" Of course, what else could he think? How could she ever begin to tell him why there was no point pursuing her dreams? That just when her number one, all-time fantasy was being dangled in front of her, she had to give it up?

Rosanna turned back to the easel and began to stab paint angrily onto the canvas, ruining all the work she'd done so far.

Andrew wasn't to be put off. "So, you're not going to Paris, why not blow off art school, come on the road with me?"

Rosanna didn't look up. "And I would be what, your groupie?"

"I was thinking more, my lover." Andrew slipped his arms around her waist as she tried to resist any feeling of warmth, any pull towards him. He turned her around to face him, his arms still circled around her. "Come on, you think Picasso went to art school?"

Rosanna sighed. Sometimes she could forget Andrew was so young. But sometimes not. "Yes. Yes, I do. At thirteen years old, Picasso was one of the youngest ever students at the Barcelona School of Fine Arts."

"Oh." Andrew looked momentarily stumped. "Well, I'm just saying, it's your life and maybe you should act like it."

"And what if it isn't my life?" Rosanna was sailing dangerously close to the edge now, but she didn't know if she cared anymore. The pain of turning down the scholarship was bad enough without Andrew coming over to rub salt in the wound.

Andrew was surly now, unhelpful. "Well, who the hell's else is it? Your dad's?"

Furiously, Rosanna pushed him away and started grabbing brushes, tidying paints. "Well, maybe it's yours, is that it? Or not. What if there is a life that I was supposed to be living, but instead I was living my life?"

"My brain hurts, woman!" Andrew rubbed his forehead in exaggerated confusion. "Do you want to go to Paris?"

"Yes!" Rosanna shouted, stunned at the level of her own passion.

"Well are you gonna go then?"

"No!"

"Why the hell not?" Andrew was close up in her face now, gripping her upper arms, almost shaking her.

Rosanna felt herself on the verge of angry, hot tears. "I can't tell you."

"You gotta tell me, Rosanna, this is crazy."

She tried to turn away from him, but he gripped her firmly, keeping her screaming into his face. "I don't have to tell you anything. This is my life."

"Well, yeah!"

They stopped, both furious, both locked in a staring contest that seemed to go on forever.

Then, suddenly, Rosanna began to laugh.

Andrew held firm for just a moment longer, but then she felt his grip on her arms loosen, and his body begin to shake as he fought the giggles rising up inside.

They slid down to the floor, helpless against the

waves of laughter that shook all the tension right out of them and brought them to their knees. They were holding on to each other now for support, not control.

"So, if you're so sure you're not going to Paris, come on the road with me."

Rosanna wiped her eyes and looked up at Andrew. "How about we talk about this after Prom?"

"You'll come away with me after Prom?" Geez, he was like a dog with a bone. Rosanna shook her head gently.

"Or you could come to Paris?" she suggested.

"And what's your dad going to think about that?"

Rosanna sighed. She'd been a single mom in charge of her own house for too long to get used to two men competing to map out her life for her.

Well, one man and one man-child.

She deflected Andrew, "Don't worry about Dad. I'll think of something."

Neither of them heard Mr. Peterson as he listened at the other side of the door that led into the house.

***

Mr. Peterson stood at the front window with the lights out, waiting for Andrew to leave.

Finally, he saw the boy duck under the half-opened garage door and head down the driveway into the dusk.

Mr. Peterson slipped out the front door, closing it silently behind him and moved fast to catch up with Andrew. As he took Andrew firmly by the arm, his smile was genial but his eyes were hard.

Andrew turned, surprised, ready to fight, but relaxed when he saw Rosanna's father. His relieved smile only seemed to make Mr. Peterson less friendly (if that were possible).

"So, Mr. McDonough, what do you think you're doing?" Mr. Peterson spat through gritted teeth.

Andrew decided to play it innocent, until he knew exactly what this was about. He affected his best meet-the-parents smile. "Mr. Peterson, I'm not sure what you mean."

"Oh, I think you know what I mean." Andrew tried hard not to wince as Mr. Peterson's grip on his arm tightened. "You just remember something. My little girl is special. She's going places and she's going to make something of her life. And you're not going to get in her way. I'm the one who's going to make sure of that."

Andrew dropped the smile, looked Mr. Peterson right in the eye and removed the hand from his arm. "Sir," he said, gently but firmly, "If I know your daughter, no one is going to get in the way of her getting what she wants."

"You think she knows what she wants yet?"

All facade of geniality was gone now as Mr. Peterson's raw fear for his daughter's future spilled out. The kind of fear only a parent could understand—something that Andrew wouldn't recognize for a long time.

"You think you know what's best?" Andrew was cocky now, self-assured. "You gonna keep her here on Walton Mountain forever? You be careful, Mr. Peterson."

He turned and walked down the driveway, into the darkness, hands in his pockets, whistling, as Mr. Peterson stared impotently after him.

***

In the garage, Rosanna stared at the canvas, seeing nothing. What if she did stay? What if she went to Paris? Would Andrew come with her? Would she find another way back to the real world and her old life?

Would Gib even miss her if she didn't?

It was hard to tell these days; she didn't think she'd got more than one syllable out of him in a year.

But she'd miss him. She'd been missing him for a long time.

15

Next morning, Julie woke and stretched lazily, luxuriously in bed. That one sweet kiss Johnnie had given her the night before still had her floating high on a haze of hormones and she wasn't ready to come down anytime soon.

Unfortunately for Julie, she was rudely interrupted as Rosanna climbed through the open bedroom window and slid to the floor with a thump!

"Jesus!" Julie sat up quickly. "What is it with this place and people climbing through windows?"

"No cell phones."

Rosanna was breezy, unperturbed as she picked herself up off of the floor. "Also, if my Dad calls, I don't want your parents to know I was here."

Seeing Julie's forehead begin to wrinkle with worry, Rosanna took her by the shoulders. "Come on beautiful, it's our last day in la-la-land and I intend to make the most of it."

Julie shifted sleepily into a stretch. "Mmm, I got that end-of-vacation, back to school feeling, know what I mean?" She opened one eye and fixed it on Rosanna. "No consequences, right?"

Rosanna grinned – Julie was in. "No consequences, my friend, so let's dine and dance for tonight we die. Any last requests?"

Julie paused, considering. "We gotta go shopping."

* * *

It was Saturday morning.

The mall was a sea of acid-wash denim as hordes of teenagers streamed into the giant, glass fronted edifice. *The Go-Go's* filtered out through tinny speakers above their heads. Guys with big hair going up the escalators flirted with the girls with even bigger hair traveling down. Beeps and flashes emanated from the arcade as twelve year old boys tanked up on Jolt Cola blasted space aliens into sprays of chunky pixels.

Julie grabbed Rosanna firmly by the arm as she started to drift towards a cute guy in a pirate hat, working the burger concession and steered her into Macy's.

"Come on, come on, come on, we gotta find that dress – it's so perfect."

"What if I don't like it?" Rosanna should have known better than to question Julie when she had that messianic glint in her eye, but... "What if my dumbass character liked it, and I hate it?"

"We'll take that risk, come on." And Julie half-led, half-dragged her into womenswear, towards the racks and racks of prom dresses - an ocean of polyester sateen glistening in a thousand shades of pastel.

Smiling wickedly, Julie began to gather up dresses into her arms, heaping some on Rosanna, keeping others just for herself.

Maybe it was the late night spent painting, but as Julie moved through the racks, she seemed to Rosanna to be moving unnaturally fast, kinda jerky, as if she'd been sped up somehow.

The ground swayed a little under Rosanna and then she blinked. Had she just missed something? They were suddenly in the middle of the department. Then it happened again – they were suddenly by the dressing room, weighed down by outfits.

Julie turned and caught her eye. She looked startled too and opened her mouth to speak but, whatever she said, Rosanna couldn't hear it. From being a background tinny annoyance, *We Got the Beat* had just gotten very, *very* LOUD!

So loud it seemed to be playing inside her head. She couldn't hear a thing. She tried to say something to the store assistant, but the woman just gave her a shiny, sticky, lipgloss smile and handed her a dressing room pass.

She blinked again and looked down.

Her lace trimmed black leggings, painters smock and ballet flats had disappeared, replaced by a blue metallic wiggle dress with a deep v-neck and enormous rosette shoulders. The music was taking her over, and she couldn't resist the urge to start dancing jerkily.

She dance-stumbled out of her cubicle to see Julie swinging the skirts of a peach sateen horror that seemed to have all the trim.

Julie was talking and now, although Rosanna couldn't exactly hear her, she found that she knew what she was saying: *What the hell is going on?*

Well, she wasn't saying anything enlightening.

Another blink and a flash and Julie was in front of her again, but this time in a black lace minidress, with matching fingerless gloves, a million rubber bangles around her wrists and her hair swept up in a messy scarf. Several large crucifixes dangled around her neck.

Julie looked up at Rosanna and burst into gales of silent laughter.

She's got some nerve thought Rosanna, until she looked down. She was in Cher's Bob Mackie *Mohawk* Oscars dress, complete with – she reached up and checked her head – giant feathered headdress.

She did the only thing she could do. She posed like the bust on the prow of a Viking ship. Then she noticed Julie was mouthing something at her; *I think we're—*

Too late. Another flash, another change. Rosanna was starting to feel seasick.

Julie was in a brown leotard and matching brown tights, with a floaty purple skirt on top. She was dancing like Kate Bush. "I can't stop! I think we're in a montage."

A montage! Now it made sense, they were stuck in a —

Another flash. Rosanna found herself in front of the mirror, in a strange bubblegum pink dress. A panel of cheap dark pink lace connected a high halter neck collar to a deep sweetheart neckline and off the shoulder sleeves. The main dress, in shiny polka-dotted satin, was baggy around the bust and waist, but hobblingly tight around the knees.

As she looked to her right, Julie was sticking her fingers down her throat. She looked back at the mirror. It looked familiar. *It couldn't be, could it be...?*

FLASH! Oh the relief! Back in front of the mirror, but this time Rosanna smiled at her reflection as she took in the form-fitting, strapless mini dress in a Basquiat-style print.

Turning towards Julie's cubicle to see her in her signature style – 50s, with a New Wave twist – the girls nodded to each other, satisfied. These were the dresses.

Suddenly the music faded back into the background,

barely audible on the store's PA, and now she could hear Julie again. "Told you it'd be your perfect dress."

***

There was no boundary to Rosanna's relief as she sat in the mall food court, shopping bags dumped at her feet and an enormous coke float on the table in front of her.

"God, is it just me, or is being in a montage kind of exhausting? It's like I actually did all that stuff, I just don't remember doing it. I need this." She took a long pull on her drink. "Still, the best part of all of this is that I can drink this, eat a burger and there's no consequences for my ass."

"Mmm," Julie agreed, "Can you remember the last time you ate or drank anything with sugar in, without feeling guilty?"

"Last time I was a teenager, I guess."

Julie smiled, but then suddenly all the color fled her face. She clutched her hand to her mouth. "Uh oh, too much ice cream."

Stumbling up from her awkward plastic seat, she disentangled her legs and ran towards the bathrooms.

***

Entering the pink and green tiled mall bathrooms, Rosanna heard retching coming from the stalls.

She walked along the row of doors, tentatively pushing each one till she found the locked one. She knocked. "Ju, you okay? It's me. I don't think anyone else is in here."

The stall door unlocked with a CLUNK and drifted

open a crack. Taking this as an invitation, Rosanna pushed back the door to find Julie doubled over the porcelain.

"You okay?" Dumb question, sure, but you gotta ask.

Julie didn't even look up from the toilet. "No, this is very definitely not okay."

"You think maybe this is some kind of post-montage motion sickness?"

Julie didn't answer, but looked nervously up at Rosanna, wiping her mouth with the back of her hand. She looked clammy and slightly green.

Pushing her way past Rosanna out the stall, she walked unsteadily out, before turning to slump against the wall. Rosanna sat on the floor opposite Julie, feeling desperately sorry for her. She looked *so* ill! She didn't push her, just waited for Julie to collect herself. She was sure to want to talk soon.

"I've seen a lot of movies."

Rosanna smiled at the non sequitur. "I know that."

"Well, there's only ever one reason a woman suddenly throws up in a movie."

"Julie?" Rosanna was confused now – where was this going?

"I'm pregnant."

Rosanna just laughed. Living in movie-land had finally fried Julie's brain. "That's nuts. How could you possibly know you're pregnant? You only had sex two days ago."

"Two days in movie time."

Rosanna still looked skeptical, but Julie didn't even pause for breath. "Come on, Rosanna, when you're watching a movie, a woman runs to the bathroom and barfs, what's the next scene?"

"She's looking at the little blue line on the test?"

"Bingo!" Julie slapped her forehead. "Oh God, I'm pregnant in a movie! My waters are gonna break over someone's shoes in the middle of an argument, instead of at the hospital like everyone else's."

Rosanna felt herself getting swept away by Julie's logic. "Well, at least if you have a movie pregnancy only your bump gets big and the rest of you stays really skinny."

She moved over to sit next to her friend and pulled Julie's head onto her shoulder, stroking her hair.

Julie attempted a watery smile. "Yeah, and I'll get my figure back the day I leave the hospital, but I still have to bitch about how big my imaginary butt is."

She looked up to see Rosanna looking at her strangely. "Ju, you're talking like you're actually going to have this baby."

Julie looked at her feet. When she spoke, her voice was small and quiet. "I can't, can I? I mean, this isn't a possibility."

Rosanna blew out her cheeks. Should she risk it? "Well, I gotta be honest, Ju, every day goes by here, I'm seeing fewer and fewer reasons to go home."

Julie's face hardened. "Yeah, well, I guess you've got everything you want here: a great dad, a great guy, an art scholarship to Paris."

Rosanna felt hurt, confused – where was all this anger suddenly coming from? "Hey, Julie, this isn't just about me. You've got someone here who really loves you. You could finally have a baby. This is what you've always wanted."

Julie scrambled to her feet. "Oh shut up, Ro! This

isn't real." She patted her stomach. "This isn't even a real baby! You can't just live here in fantasy la la-land."

Rosanna was on her feet too now. "*I'm* living in fantasyland? What about you? You really think Roger's ever gonna give you kids? That you're happily married? That he loves you?"

Julie faltered. "He does want kids, just—"

Rosanna cut her off – she'd been listening to excuses about how Roger wasn't 'ready' for over ten years now, and she'd had it up to her eyeballs.

"Roger is just waiting you out. Don't you get it? He knows you've always wanted kids and he's just sitting back and keeping you waiting until all your eggs just shrivel up one by one and go pop, pop, pop!"

Furious, Julie regained her momentum. "Don't try and bullshit me just because you want to stay! This place is perfect for you; everything's just handed to you on a plate by your dad or your boyfriend. You never have to get a life of your own and you can be a big kid forever, just like you always wanted."

"Yeah, well if being a grown up like you means being married to Roger the Man-child, you can stick it!"

Julie began furiously snatching up shopping bags and made for the exit. "Come on, you're the one who said there were no consequences and you were right. I'm going home and this never happened."

"And what if I was wrong?"

Julie stopped mid-stride, but she didn't turn back. Rosanna kept talking to the back of her head. "What if there *are* consequences? You're just going to leave Johnnie and all this for dust? Or for Roger?"

Julie wavered, but still didn't turn. "Let's just stick to

the script. We're meeting Johnnie at the beach."

"Fine, I'll just go call Andrew, tell him to meet us there."

This time Julie did turn around. She fixed Rosanna with a ten-mile stare. "Andrew? You guys were supposed to break up. Now you're messing with the story – you never think about anyone else!"

"*I'm* messing with the story?" Rosanna choked down a laugh. "Johnnie's supposed to still be in love with me, and taking *me* to the Prom, not making babies with *you*."

"Shit." Julie kicked the wall – not a good idea in jelly shoes. "Ouch!"

"See what I mean? Things have already changed." Rosanna's tone was gentle now, cajoling. "We could still stay here."

Julie gave her a look, and it might have just been the broken toe, but it wasn't a friendly look.

"Well, I could stay here. You do what you want. Come on." Rosanna picked up her shopping bags and barged past Julie out of the bathroom.

16

Julie leaned on her arm out the open window of Rosanna's newly acquired lipstick-pink VW Karmann Ghia.

Another bribe to stay home with Daddy Peterson, no doubt.

The sun hurt her eyes and the wind scraped her skin as she watched strip malls whip past, but she wanted to be as far away as possible from Rosanna while still sitting in the same damn car.

Who did Rosanna think she was, to spend all that time and effort convincing her that there were no consequences? That nothing here meant anything and then – when Julie had gotten herself into this much trouble – to just turn around and say maybe it *did* matter?

And what about what she'd said about Roger? Is that what she'd been thinking about him all these years? That he was stringing her along, waiting until she was too old to have kids?

Just thinking about it, Julie felt an ache deep down where she'd longed for years to feel a baby of her own.

Where even now, maybe that wished-for baby was finally growing... But no, that was silly, this baby was as fictional as everything else in this place.

Absent-mindedly she stroked her belly, trying not to imagine that it already felt a little rounder.

And what if things were different, if this were Roger's baby? Had he ever dreamed of raising a family with her, really? If she thought about it honestly....

No, Julie wasn't ready yet to think about what Rosanna had said honestly.

But no matter how hard she pushed it down, no matter how much she focused on her anger with Rosanna, the things she'd said about Roger sat there, throbbing like a bad tooth; something that she knew she'd have to deal with sometime.

Just not right now.

***

Rosanna was a ball of confusion. God, she was sorry.

But then again, she really wasn't.

How long had she been listening to Julie make excuses for Roger? It almost made her own husband look like he'd done the decent thing – he gave her a child (okay, by accident, but a happy one for her) and then he left, so she never even got the chance to have to ask herself if she should stay with him for the sake of the child, or her wedding vows or anything else.

Sure, it had burned at the time and being a single mom was no picnic, but it had to beat being shackled to a man you couldn't respect anymore.

And that, really, was why she was so mad at Julie. It wasn't just that it was obvious that Roger didn't respect her. It was more that she didn't believe Julie could really, deep down respect him.

And who could live with that?

***

Rosanna brought the car to a screeching halt in a parking spot overlooking the beach. The place was packed with kids enjoying the late afternoon sun.

Johnnie was already waiting, him and his bike leaning on the boardwalk rail. He pushed himself off, keeping his hands deep in his jacket pockets in an affectation of cool and strolled over to greet the girls.

Seeing Julie emerge from the passenger door, all pretense of cool was forgotten as he rushed to take both her hands and help her out, bringing her up close, face to face.

All the tension of the car ride, the row with Rosanna, the worries about the future were pushed out as excitement fizzed through every vein and crackled out, spilling over her skin, to be so close to him.

"Hey Principessa," he whispered and kissed her gently.

"Hey." Julie's head reeled from the kiss. He gave her a slow, secret smile to show he understood and then, remembering his manners, he turned to greet Rosanna. "Hey Rosanna, what's up?"

Rosanna had grabbed Julie's bags of shopping from the back seat of the Ghia and was stuffing them into the trunk, taking out her frustration on the purchases. "Hey Johnnie, just packing for a long trip."

She grinned harshly and Johnnie, sensing the weird vibe pouring off her, looked to Julie. "Everything okay with you guys?"

"Yeah, well, sure…" Julie's buzz started to wear off as she saw Rosanna, still obviously fuming. Determined to hang on to what was good on this final day, she turned back to Johnnie. "Hey, it's our last day here on Planet Earth, remember? What do you want to do?"

"Come on, I'll show you." He took her hand and led her down to the beach.

* * *

Rosanna watched as Johnnie led Julie down to the water's edge. So absorbed was she that she didn't notice Andrew's Oldsmobile pull up a couple of spaces down. Sneaking up behind her, he followed her gaze out to sea.

Rosanna jumped as an arm snaked around her waist, then turned to see Andrew and relaxed back into his embrace.

She looked back to Julie and Johnnie: Julie was taking off her shoes and then, catching her off balance, Johnnie took them from her and whipped her up into his arms, carrying her with mock-Herculean effort. Julie laughed and kissed him on the nose.

"He really loves her, doesn't he?" It was as though Andrew was the voice of her thoughts.

"Uh-huh," she agreed. She'd never seen Julie so truly loved before, so cherished. And she could see Julie opening up in the warmth of that love. That had to be real, didn't it?

* * *

As the boys played Frisbee, Julie and Rosanna lay back on beach towels, eyes hidden by imitation Ray-Bans. They hadn't spoken since they hit the sand.

Finally Julie broke the silence: "Can I ask you something?"

"If I tell you what I really think, are you gonna listen?"

Julie sighed. "It's nothing like that it's just... What's it like, really, having a kid?"

Rosanna blew her cheeks out – whatever she said here had to be wrong, right?

If she said it was great, she was encouraging Julie to do the wrong thing. If she said it was hard work, she'd just be trying to put her off. Maybe she'd try the unvarnished truth...

"It's hell. Absolute hell from the day they pop out."

"Oh." Julie had no idea how to respond to this. "Oh, um, but you love him, right?"

Rosanna considered how to put it. "Sure, of course I love him, but it's... Think about the worst guy you ever dated, the most inconsiderate, most selfish son of a bitch, but at the time you were crazy about him, right?"

"Um, yeah, John Westwood, 1994." Julie didn't have to dig too far to dredge up the guy who matched that description. She gave a little shudder at the memory.

"Oh God, yeah." Rosanna remembered that one too – what a tool.

"Well, that's exactly what having a baby is like. They don't care about you, your needs, what you want, how much it costs you to give them what they need, as long as they get it. But you will absolutely adore them, you can't help it."

"But there is an upside, right?"

Rosanna looked at Julie's anxious face and smiled. She wouldn't be fair to Julie if she didn't let her know that yes, there was the biggest upside.

"Oh, that's just the first year. After that, they are amazing. Everything in their world is fresh and it's beautiful and they think you're amazing too."

Rosanna stretched herself back on the towel and looked up to the sky. "Your heart expands with so much love, more than you ever thought you'd feel. Every whisper, every heartbeat, every goddam snotty nose is a miracle that only you get to see."

She smiled and closed her eyes, holding the memory of Gib as a baby close.

Opening them again, she saw Julie was looking at her, a strange expression on her face. "Yeah?"

"Yeah. Of course, then they turn into teenagers and then it all goes to hell again. But when Gib was a baby, I remember even just his feet were just so amazing. Like every morning, I'd be looking at the curve of his instep and it was the most beautiful, most perfect thing I'd ever seen."

Julie looked at Rosanna, lost in her own world, and sighed. "Gib was a gorgeous baby."

"He's still my gorgeous baby. He's the love of my life." Rosanna pushed herself up on her elbows and looked out to sea. "I gotta go home, don't I?"

Julie didn't answer – it wasn't really a question.

Rosanna snapped out a bubble of gum and smiled wryly. "I knew it. Well, I guess I always knew it, but I just wanted to put it off and live in the fantasy a little while longer, you know?"

"Hey Rosanna," Julie touched her friend's arm, getting her full attention for the first time in a while. "You know those guys, you love them and they treat you like shit?"

Rosanna squinted at her through the sunglasses, waiting for her to continue.

"Well, sometimes even the nicest guys will treat you as badly as you let them get away with."

"Hah!" Rosanna stared back out to sea. "Right back atcha, honey."

"Touché."

"What's that about your tush?" The boys bounded

over and threw themselves down on the sand. Johnnie flipped Julie onto her front. "Come on, let's inspect it!"

"Get off!" Julie was laughing and trying to slap him away.

Seeing that they were lost in their own world, Andrew turned to Rosanna. "So, are we still on for tonight?"

"Sure, why wouldn't we be?"

"Well, your Dad, is he okay with this?"

Rosanna prickled. One thing she'd forgotten about being a teenager was how often you had to explain yourself. Or not.

"I'm kind of planning on getting ready at Julie's." She pushed her sunglasses further back, completely hiding her eyes.

Andrew looked at her – she could see the cogs whirring as he chose his words. "Seriously, your Dad's a good guy. He's just a little over-protective of you."

Enough already! Rosanna rolled over and looked straight up at Andrew. "Seriously? I am not missing Prom. It is literally life and death, and I am not arguing with you about this, young man."

Oops – maybe she'd gone a bit too far at the end there. She saw Andrew visibly flinch at the *young man*. "Well, now you're creeping me out, *Mom*."

Too bad, thought Rosanna and rolling back onto her back, she shook herself out in the sun, ignoring Andrew.

Out of the corner of her eye, she could see him struggling with whether to say more, but luckily he must have decided to drop it, and turned to look out to sea.

Gotta get home, thought Rosanna, gotta get home. This place looked like a dream, but it turned out it wasn't as easy as it looked – when everything was handed to you on a plate, it all seemed to come with strings.

Julie's plan to get home had better work…

17

The sun was setting in a burnt orange sky as Rosanna's car pulled up in front of Julie's house. Andrew, coming in behind them, hung a u-turn and pulled up beside her, driver to driver side. Rosanna leaned out her open window and kissed Andrew full on the lips.

Andrew pulled back and gave her a meaningful look. "Okay, I'll see you there. Talk to your dad."

Rosanna dropped back into her car with a plump. "Yeah, I'll definitely think about that. See you later!" She waved without making eye contact and – after a moment – Andrew took the hint and drove away.

The girls got out of the car and just as Rosanna was opening the trunk to take out their shopping, the front door to Julie's house opened and out came Doug, Iona…and Mr. Peterson.

He did not look happy.

"Uh oh." Julie locked eyes with Rosanna.

"We have got to get to the Prom." Rosanna slammed the trunk shut again and whipped around to the driver's door.

As she scrabbled with the handle, she saw Julie, still frozen to the spot as the parents advanced towards them. "Come on!"

Diving into the driver seat, she leaned across and jerked open the passenger door, purposefully banging Julie on the butt, hard.

"Ow!" Back to her senses, Julie turned and jumped in the car.

As Rosanna peeled away from the curb, Julie wound

down the window and stuck her head out, shouting back into the wind: "We're really sorry. Um, I'll explain later!" She plopped back down into her seat.

"No you won't."

Julie wound her hair tight around her fingers. "I know, I...I guess I just needed something to say." She looked in the side mirror at the image of her parents getting smaller and smaller. This would be the last time she'd ever see them.

Rosanna flicked a glance to the side and saw Julie's anxious, unhappy face. Shit, she couldn't afford for Julie to go all wobbly on her now. "We just have to make a pit stop for emergency make-up supplies and then we're on the home straight, right?"

"Right, yeah. The home straight." Julie didn't look round, still staring at the now vacant side mirror.

***

In the school bathrooms, Rosanna scrunch-dried her hair under the hand dryer. From her upside-down vantage point, she watched as Julie touched up her lipgloss one more time, then smoothed her dress, rubbing her hand over the imagined round of her belly, pulling the dress a little tighter where the bump would soon appear.

If there were to be a bump, that is.

Hair finished, she walked over to the mirror and put her arm around her friend's shoulder, giving her a squeeze that she hoped was reassuring. "Better than mortal man deserves."

"Hah." Julie attempted a watery smile. "Come on, let's go."

* * *

Emerging from the bathroom, Julie and Rosanna were swept up in a tide of teenagers, all heading for the gym at the end of the hall.

As they entered the gym, Julie gasped.

Banners and pennants hung from the walls and above them loomed a giant net of balloons, waiting to be released at the end of the night.

Up on stage, a woman sang cheesy power rock while attired in what seemed to be some cruel cross between saran wrap and tinfoil. Behind her back-up band (all keyboards), the yearbook video was projected on a large pull-down screen.

From the edge of the dancefloor, she could see young girls in pastel taffetas bop self-consciously with skinny boys in ill-fitting tuxes; teachers were surreptitiously slipping booze from hip flasks into their soft drinks; Geeks and Zoids lurked in the darker corners – one of them even seemed to be wearing night vision goggles.

But it wasn't that the scene, the people, the band or even the décor were so amazing. It was just that it looked *exactly* like the movie. Julie gazed around, open-mouthed, until Rosanna nudged her in the ribs, hard.

She turned to see what the problem was, rubbing her side in exaggerated pain.

"So what do we do now?" Rosanna was scanning the room, crackling with nervous energy. "Do we just find a VCR and stick a fork in it?"

She grabbed a dessert fork from the nearest table, not even noticing the people sitting there, who all ducked as she swept her arm overhead, miming the stabbing motion as she talked. "Just stick the fork right in?"

"No!" Julie grabbed her arm. "No, there's this one song playing when it happens. You remember that song?"

Rosanna was looking at her blankly – Geez, why couldn't she have ever watched this movie? "Such a great song. Oh God, what is it called? I can hear it. I can hear it."

"Can you hear it right now? Cause that would help."

Julie was gesturing wildly, twirling her hands in the air, sticking out her tongue in forced concentration. "No, Geez... oh, it's on the tip of my brain, ahh—"

Rosanna's eyes were almost popping out of her head from the force of willing Julie to remember.

Julie's hands flew to her temples, like a guy in an old black and white movie attempting a mind-reading trick. Then suddenly she relaxed. Rosanna looked at her, expectantly.

"No, it's gone. But I will definitely know it when I hear it."

"That's...reassuring. Come on, let's go find this—" Leading Julie away from the dancefloor, her plan was cut short as they turned smack into Andrew and Johnnie.

Andrew was looking sharp in a classic black tux... and battered Converse sneakers.

Johnnie was quirky as ever in a more deluxe version of his usual rockabilly style. He pulled down the velvet cuffs of his midnight blue drape jacket and straightened his bolo tie nervously in its faux-onyx clip.

"Well, ladies, what can I say? Julie, that is a truly volcanic ensemble."

Julie smiled, her whole body melting towards Johnnie, when suddenly Andrew cut into her line of vision. "May I have this dance?"

"Um, why, sure. Okay" Julie looked over Andrew's shoulder as she took his outstretched hand, but Johnnie just smiled and shrugged, so she let herself be led onto the dancefloor.

Left alone and momentarily nonplussed, Johnnie and Rosanna turned to one another. Johnnie gave a small, courtly bow. "May I?"

He held out his hand to Rosanna and they took their place among the ungainly teenage couples on the dancefloor, where Johnnie immediately surprised – and unbalanced – Rosanna by throwing her into a twirl and snapping her straight back.

Allowing herself to be shuffled around by Andrew, Julie caught Rosanna's eye. More connected than they had been since their row in the mall bathrooms, they understood exactly what the other was thinking.

This was just plain wrong.

With a laugh and a shrug, the girls steered their partners towards each other and engineered a graceful swap. Julie fell immediately into Johnnie's fast steps and turns, while Rosanna was relieved to settle into the side-to-side bopping she'd perfected in her teens the first time around.

Getting her breath back, Rosanna looked over at Johnnie as he pulled Julie from a turn, back into his arms. She saw Julie laughing in pure joy.

Andrew followed her gaze, watching Julie and Johnnie as their jive steps got ever more complicated. "Oh no, I know my limits. The side-step shuffle is all you get."

Rosanna laughed at the misunderstanding. "Believe me, I can live with that."

"Well, maybe not all you get." She shrieked as Andrew suddenly dipped her back almost to the ground, his lips closing on hers as the blood rushed to her head.

* * *

Across the dancefloor, Andrew's romantic gesture had caught Johnnie's eye. He gasped in mock horror, "That guy is stealing all my moves!"

Julie grinned and thumped him gently on the shoulder.

"Oh, it's okay," he reassured her, "I got moves to spare."

"That you do." Julie nestled close against him, caught in bittersweet confusion. She longed just to enjoy this moment, to forget what was to come, but she couldn't and she couldn't tell him.

Johnnie's voice broke into her thoughts. "Does this really feel like the end of high school to you?"

"Does it ever!" Julie burst out with more feeling than consideration. "I thought at one point I was never gonna get out of here."

"That bad?" Johnnie looked down at her in amused surprise. "I thought you lived for school, couldn't get enough of the old study hall."

Julie lifted her hand, a mock threat to thump him again. Then relaxing back into the slow dance, she considered her reply.

"No. Not all bad. Just, it's time to get out into the real world, you know what I mean?" She didn't know why she was asking, even rhetorically.

But Johnnie was smiling down at her, his face full of love and hope and trust. "Yeah, I think I know what you mean. Now."

Her heart broke a little more as she understood. Johnnie saw the real world unfolding before them full of the promise of a brilliant future, of love, of them.

Seeing in his eyes his vulnerability and his total fearlessness in the face of love, it hurt to look, to know that she was the one who would destroy his dreams.

She looked away. "Oh God, I've been dying to get out of here and now I never want this night to end."

"But it has to end, Jules." Wildly, her eyes snapped back to his face. What did he know?

But when she looked up, he was smiling. "It's your last night on earth, remember? Come midnight, the planet explodes and only those with their own private rocket ship survive."

"Huh, Scooter'll be okay then." Feeling tears prick her eyes, she buried her face in his warm, solid shoulder.

Then, suddenly, it hit her.

Churning, rolling sickness hit her, that is. She stood straight up, backing away from Johnnie.

"You okay, Principessa?"

She stumbled, clutching her stomach. "No. I gotta go to the bathroom."

Julie turned and ran, pushing through the crowded dancefloor, ignoring the startled 'heys' and one 'what a bitch!' in her determination to get to a stall before anyone saw her hurl.

***

A long time later, Johnnie sat at a table on the edge of the dancefloor and looked at his watch. Should he go look for Julie?

He'd already been caught in the girls' bathroom once this school year and that wasn't even his fault – there was just one tiny little misunderstanding and next thing he knew, some meathead was shoving him in the ladies. Totally different experience to the guys' bathroom – everything smelled good, and they even had a candy machine in there! *A candy machine!*

Maybe it was no wonder Julie spent so long in there. Still...

His face lit up in relief as Rosanna appeared and sat herself down at his table.

"Well, Rosanna, I think I have a confession to make."

"Oh yeah?" She gave him a smile that would once have left him tongue-tied and twisted, but now he had something he needed to tell her about that.

"See, it's like this. I know I pledged my absolute, undying love to you. But it kinda turns out it wasn't as undying as I thought."

Rosanna laughed, looking at his oh-so-serious face. "Johnnie, what was that, like seventh grade?"

"I know, I know, I just don't want you thinking I make a habit of inconstancy."

Rosanna knew where this was going, but she couldn't help teasing him a little longer. She raised her eyebrows in a questioning gesture and waited for him to continue.

"See, you love the Jules, I know you do." Johnnie didn't need to wait for Rosanna to agree. "And I love the Jules. And I just want you to know, I am never going to hurt her."

Rosanna smiled. Who could not love this guy? Well, not like that, not her anyway, but right now she just wanted to put him in her pocket and adopt him.

She reached out a hand and ruffled his hair. "If only

guys like you existed in the real world.

Johnnie ducked his head in embarrassment and changed the subject. "Geez, the real world, here it comes."

"Got any plans?"

Johnnie paused, his blush deepening to a flaming red and looked at his hands.

"You really do love her, don't you?"

Johnnie's head snapped up. "Well, yeah. I thought I made that pretty clear."

"And you'd do anything to make her happy, to give her what she wants?"

"Of course." Johnnie's eyes drifted away as he pondered a lifetime of making Julie happy.

Rosanna watched him, considering her next words carefully. She knew Julie would always do what she believed to be the right thing, but what if the wrong thing was the right thing all along?

Maybe Julie just needed a little extra help...

But Johnnie was the first to break the pause. "Speaking of Julie, she's a real long time in the bathroom. Could you go check on her?"

This was her chance; she had to say something. As she hesitated, Johnnie spoke again, "Rosanna? Some jobs I just can't do…"

Taking a deep breath, she spelled her next words out deliberately.

"Well, she's probably throwing up again. I mean, that's what happens when you're having a baby."

Rosanna watched Johnnie, waiting for the bomb to go off.

It took some time.

As he sat, slack-jawed with amazement, Andrew

reappeared with their drinks and Rosanna seized her chance to escape, putting the drinks down on the table and steering Andrew onto the dancefloor.

When you drop a bomb, it's often a good idea not to stick around.

"Hey! It took me an eon to get those drinks!" Then Andrew noticed Johnnie, still staring into space with his mouth open. "Is he alright?"

Johnnie made a noise. It sounded like 'Hnh?'

"Sure, he just had some good news, is all." Rosanna moved briskly away through the heaving mass of dancers, taking Andrew with her.

Andrew looked like he was going to start asking more questions, so she distracted him by drawing him in real close.

It didn't entirely distract him. "You look suspiciously pleased with yourself."

"Well, I think I just did my good deed for the day. Maybe the century."

"You want to tell me about it?"

"No." She snuggled in close to him, blissfully content. "I'm so happy. I should get home before I change my mind."

"About what, coming away with me?" He drew back from her again, looking concerned.

This was no good, thought Rosanna. She was on a high from her meddling in Julie's life, and now she just wanted to get back to enjoying the glow before real life came and smacked her on the ass.

She brushed him off. "Yeah, something like that."

"Rosanna, you did square everything with your Dad, didn't you, about coming to Prom?"

"Sure, sure. It's all fine" She nestled back into his shoulder.

"Well good, because he's here right now."

Rosanna's head snapped up. There, at the edge of the dancefloor, was Mr. Peterson, scanning the crowd. Their eyes locked.

"Oh shit." Looking around for an escape route, Rosanna could see nothing.

18

Out in the darkened corridor, Julie stumbled out of the girls' bathroom to find a stony-faced Johnnie leaning against the wall opposite, his arms folded.

"When were you going to tell me, Julie?"

"What?" Julie's mind raced. What did he mean? Had he discovered who she really was? Where she was from? Then she realized the secret he was more likely to believe.

"Oh crap. I'm gonna kill Rosanna!"

Johnnie wasn't to be deflected. "You weren't going to tell me?"

Julie sighed, too worn out from her recent bout of vomiting to argue her case or make something up. "Oh Johnnie, what would be the point? I can't have this baby."

"The point?" Johnnie's face twisted in something she had never seen there before – anger. "The *POINT*? The point is I love you! The point is - I thought you loved me."

All the pain that she had imagined inflicting on him, out there on the dancefloor, it was all etched across his face.

She had thought it would be bad to leave him behind in the innocent belief that they'd be together, that she could hardly bear the guilt of leaving him to bear it on his own, but seeing this was much, much worse. "I do love you," she protested weakly.

"So we should be in this together. We should be

deciding this together." His words fell like hammer blows. "I'm busy building my whole future around you, Julie, and okay, maybe babies weren't part of that plan yet, but I don't care because I figured we have our whole lives to work it out and I thought you felt the same way!"

Julie felt her whole body was weighted with a hundred tons of misery, dragging her to the ground. "You really think it's that simple?"

"It *is* that simple!"

She stepped towards him, stretching out a hand in front of her. She longed to comfort him, but his words were killing her. How could everything just seem so straightforward to him?

But that was Johnnie all over, she realized. He fell in love, he wanted to be with you, and that was all there was. No games, no secrets, no lies.

Seeing all that she couldn't have in front of her, she felt hot tears running down her face.

Johnnie's anger relented and he put his arms around her, drawing her in. "I'm sorry, I just, I live to love you, Jules. And if you won't let me do that, I don't know what else there is."

He pulled her in even closer, sliding a hand over her belly. "And if there's a little Julie in there, I think I could learn to love her too."

The comfort of his arms, of his love, was irresistible. Julie looked up, attempting a watery smile. "Or a little Johnnie?"

The moment she said it, she just wanted to cram her fist into her mouth and choke herself. She couldn't let herself keep getting sucked into this ridiculous fantasy. "That was stupid... Johnnie, you know we can't have a baby."

"Well, if the world doesn't end tonight, will you think about it?"

At last, a promise she could keep. "Okay, if the world doesn't end tonight, I will definitely give it some consideration."

"You promise?"

Julie pushed him, half-smiling through the tears. "Shut up. I'm sorry Johnnie..."

But she never got the chance to try to explain anything. Footsteps came echoing down the empty hall and they both looked up to see Andrew, agitated and upset.

Probably had a row with Rosanna, Julie was guessing.

"Hey Andrew," Julie smiled, hoping he wouldn't notice her tear-streaked face. Maybe if this was a movie, it wouldn't turn bright red and swell up like a bullfrog, like it usually did every time she cried.

"Where's Rosanna? I kinda need to kill her slowly and then we need to talk."

"Rosanna's gone."

At Andrew's words, Julie's whole body blenched in shock. "Was there an accident? Did she use a fork?"

Andrew looked at her in total confusion. "What? No, her Dad showed up. He's taking her home right now."

"Oh no!" Julie was on her feet in an instant, leaving Andrew and Johnnie staring after her as she ran for the doors that led out to the parking lot.

* * *

Racing out the double doors, Julie screeched to a halt as she saw Rosanna and her dad in the middle of a knockdown, drag-out argument, right in the middle of the parking lot.

Like anxious referees, her own parents and the school principal, Mr. Donnelly, hovered round the edges. Mr. Peterson had his hand on Rosanna's arm and was half-dragging her to his car.

As she got nearer, she could make out some of what was being said – Rosanna's voice was clear enough, but Mr. Peterson was muttering. "Just get in the car, Rosanna. You're embarrassing me."

"You don't understand! I have to go back into the Prom!"

Mr. Donnelly tentatively tried to intervene, clearing his throat heavily. "Er, Rosanna, I'm afraid we cannot allow any student to attend the Prom who has been forbidden by their parents, um, their parent, yes."

He cleared his throat again, gave a 'hem' and then stepped back, obviously feeling he had said all that ever needed to be said on the subject.

Iona, Doug, and Rosanna all looked up as Julie crept onto the scene. Julie's heartache increased as the Placids looked at her with disappointment in their eyes, but Rosanna's expression was pleading for help. Julie had to take charge of the situation for once.

"Please, Mr. Peterson. It's just this one night and it's really important."

Iona put her hand firmly on Julie's arm. "Julie, stop. This is between Rosanna and her dad. When you're a bit older, you'll understand."

"Not too soon, I hope." Julie heard Doug muttering under his breath.

Julie looked beseechingly at Mr. Peterson and

thought that she could see him start to soften a little, when she heard a scuffling behind her on the grass verge. Mr. Peterson looked over her shoulder and his gaze hardened again.

Looking around she saw Andrew, brought up short by Mr. Peterson's obvious anger, Johnnie slamming into his back.

"Well, look who's here." Julie could practically taste Mr. Peterson's fury as he rounded again on Rosanna. "Was it his idea for you to lie to me and sneak out of my house?"

"Mr. Peterson, I..." Andrew was lost, out of his depth.

"No!" Rosanna pushed back now, with a fury to match Mr. Peterson's. She turned to Andrew, "You stay out of this."

Then all her focus was back on her father. "This has nothing to do with him."

"And that's what you'll be saying when you're knocked up by this...this beatnik and he's hitched a ride out of your life!" Mr. Peterson's anger looked dangerously close to turning to tears.

"Oh, you'd love that, wouldn't you?" Andrew burst in. "You could keep her at home forever then!"

"Rosanna's got a place at the Chicago Institute. She's going to have a life!"

"Damn right," Andrew shot back. "She's going to have a real life, with me, seeing America."

"Both of you *SHUT UP!*" Rosanna screamed. Mr. Peterson and Andrew turned to look at her, almost seeming surprised to see her still there.

Rosanna took a deep breath and resisted the urge to

smack them both. "I won't be staying in Chicago. But Andrew, I'm not coming with you either. I have to work out how to do this for myself."

And as she blew the air, and the anger out through her lips, she realized that it was true.

Mr. Peterson turned to her in confusion. He looked defeated and suddenly smaller. "You're going to Paris?"

"Something like that."

Mr. Peterson tried to summon back some of the righteous anger that had filled him just moments earlier, but all he could seem to manage was flustered and upset. "You're... you're too young. I'm—You'll fly off to Paris, and then you'll spend all your vacations sailing the Mediterranean or backpacking across Europe and I'll practically never see you again."

All fight gone, his voice started to crack and falter. "Geez, I tried so hard to be a friend to you and I end up sounding just like any other dad."

Wishing desperately that she had a good explanation, Rosanna moved towards him and put her arms around his neck. "But Daddy, I can't stay here while you live my life for me. I have to leave sometime."

"What now? Forever? You're only eighteen."

Andrew, smarting from Rosanna's rejection of his grand plans, just couldn't help himself from butting in again. "She's old enough."

Mr. Peterson turned to Andrew, his anger flaring up again and Rosanna could see her small hope of a reasonable discussion slipping away. "She told you to stay out of this." He jabbed a finger at Rosanna. "Get in the car, now. We're going home to sort this out."

Deep in despair, Julie was suddenly distracted as she

heard the first bars of a strangely familiar song drift from the high windows of the gym. Was it? Was this the song she'd been waiting to hear?

As *If You Leave* by Orchestral Manoeuvres in the Dark continued to play, she was sure – this was the song.

With no time to lose, she ran over and grabbed Rosanna by the arm. "Rosanna!" she hissed, "we got to go, now!"

Confused for a moment, Rosanna's expression changed to understanding as she heard the music. "This is it? This is the song?"

"Yes. Now. Run now." Julie's hand tightened its grip on Rosanna's arm as she started to run back to the school, leaving the assembled adults to stare after them.

Iona sighed. "Oh Julie."

19

The girls raced into the gym, Rosanna looking around wildly. "Where's this VCR?"

"It must be near the stage – come on!" Julie grabbed Rosanna by the hand and half-dragged her through the crowded dancefloor to where the band was playing.

Spotting a red curtain to the side of the stage, Julie dove through, pulling Rosanna behind her.

There, wired into the wall, was a top-loading Betamax VCR.

"Yes!" Rosanna reached into her purse and pulled out a dessert fork.

"Oh, okay. You just held onto that?"

But Rosanna wasn't listening, she was already busy pressing all the buttons on the VCR. "So, how did you do this before? I just flip up the deck and stick it in?"

As Julie peered nervously out through the curtain, she saw the yearbook video flicker, and then stop. Her heart nearly stopped too, sure that all attention would now be on the little alcove that housed the VCR but, although people looked up, the music continued, and so did the dancing.

Julie let out the breath she'd been holding and turned to Rosanna. Her stomach flipped as she saw that Rosanna was ready, the top deck open and fork poised, ready to plunge it into the machine.

She looked Rosanna in the eye, seeing her own nerves reflected back to her, and took the free hand that was offered to her. "Okay, I'm ready."

Rosanna raised her arm high above her head. Her grip on Julie's hand tightened till all their finger bones crunched together, and they both closed their eyes, screwing their faces up tight in anticipation of being electrocuted.

Rosanna unscrewed one eye, took aim and thrust the fork hard into the VCR.

And...

And…..

20

Nothing.

Opening her eyes, Julie could still see the alcove with the VCR in front of them, could still hear OMD. "I don't understand."

Rosanna started to stab the fork into the VCR, over and over. "This damn stupid machine! WHY. WON'T. YOU. WORK?!"

Julie's panic rose as, through a gap in the curtains, she saw Mr. Peterson, her parents, Andrew, and Johnnie enter the gym, looking around for her and Rosanna. "Oh Rosanna, hurry! We don't have much time."

"Well, that depends on how you define 'time'."

Hearing Scooter's voice behind her, Julie jumped about a foot in the air, yanking Rosanna away from the Betamax.

How had he appeared from the back of the alcove, where there was no door or window? That creepy little…

"Oh Christ, Scooter, you scared the living shit out of me!"

Scooter smirked. He looked annoyingly superior, though Julie couldn't for the life of her think why. "I found something and I thought you might need it." From behind his back, he produced a Betamax videotape.

In fact, it was *the* videotape – Julie's very own home recording of *If You Leave* with the title Sharpied on in her own handwriting, and her little gold star stickers stuck all over, from all those years ago.

Rosanna dropped the fork, dumbstruck.

Julie grabbed the tape from Scooter's hands. "Where...? How did you get this?"

How could this have traveled from their reality, when their clothes, their jewelry – even their own faces – hadn't made the journey?

Scooter took an excruciatingly long pause – the still, smug center of calm in contrast to the nervous energy crackling from Julie and Rosanna.

He drew a theatrical breath and finally began to speak, punctuating with exaggerated flourishes of his small hands.

"The night before you replaced my sister, I was conducting my own practical research into pan-dimensional travel."

A thought made Julie pause in her disbelief: "Were you experimenting on Muffin again?"

"The cat?" Rosanna was having her own pause, but Scooter seemed unruffled.

"The test subject was unharmed. In fact, I believed the experiment to be entirely unsuccessful at that time. However..." Scooter coughed self-importantly.

"After your own attempted foray into black hole exploration, I found this tape in my room. It made for interesting viewing. I had no idea that something as primitive as Betamax technology would be the missing component of my research."

Listening to this strange, pompous ten year old boy, Julie was overwhelmed by a rush of affection. Maybe it was the pregnancy hormones, but the reality of leaving even this smallest, oddest member of her fictional family behind pierced her heart.

She scooped him up in a bone-crushing hug. "Oh Scoots, I'm going to miss you, you little weirdo!"

Embarrassed but resigned, Scooter endured the hug until Rosanna, unable to stand the delay any longer, whipped the tape out of his hand.

"Okay, that's great, tick tock, let's go!" Julie might feel she had time to get lost in bittersweet goodbyes, but Rosanna had her own family – Gib – to get back to.

She slammed the tape into the VCR deck and it started to play…

* * *

Pushing through the dancefloor crowd, Andrew was distracted as one by one, the students around him stopped dancing and looked up at the screen above the stage.

On the screen was the school gym, filled with students dancing at their Prom, just like now.

Was it a live feed? Some of the students obviously thought so, as they waved upwards to some unseen camera, watching in vain to see themselves wave back.

Then the picture changed, and Andrew felt a cold pall of confusion wash over him as he saw himself. He was on the dancefloor talking to Rosanna.

But the words coming from his mouth were ones that he'd never said.

The onscreen Andrew was holding Rosanna tightly, as if preventing her escape. "It's okay if you don't believe in me. But I need you to believe in you."

The onscreen Rosanna's eyes filled with tears. "And you think a stupid video can just fix everything?"

He watched as she pulled out of this other Andrew's grip and turned to run past the side of the stage, ducking through a red velvet curtain.

Andrew's eyes snapped from the screen to the real curtain at the side of the stage and saw Julie, staring back at him in panic. Behind her was Rosanna, her back to him, messing with some VCR.

Julie snapped the curtain shut.

As he ran towards the curtain, Johnnie, Mr, Peterson, Iona and Doug – who had been similarly transfixed by the strange video – saw him go and started to follow.

***

Holding the flimsy curtains tight shut behind her, Julie screamed in her panic. "Come on, they've seen us! We've got to go!"

"The fork. I can't find the damn fork!" Rosanna was scrabbling her hand down the side of the VCR.

Julie looked around frantically. "There! There on the floor." She pointed at the glinting object, still holding the curtains with the other hand.

Rosanna dove down, grabbed the fork with one hand, then shot up and grabbed Julie with the other.

As she yanked Julie, the curtains fell apart and they could see the images on the big screen strobe and flicker as the tracking failed. Smoke began to creep from the VCR.

The girls looked up at the screen, then at each other. "You ready?" Rosanna whispered.

Julie didn't answer, distracted as Andrew burst through the curtain, followed by Johnnie, then her parents and Mr. Peterson. She looked at Johnnie, then back at Rosanna.

"I just don't know. I want this baby."

"Baby!?" Iona's face crumpled with shock, but the girls were oblivious to the mayhem and confusion around them.

The air seemed still as an empty church as Rosanna looked Julie in the eye, waiting for her answer. "It's now or never."

Rosanna steeled herself, raising the fork high above her head and plunged it deep into the VCR.

In that last split second, Julie let go of Rosanna's hand.

21

Julie would never forget that smile. The last look that Rosanna ever gave her, before the force of the electrocution blew them both across the tiny room and into the wall, leaving everything after that in darkness. It was a smile of understanding, of a lifetime of friendship...

And just the teeniest, tiniest hint of triumph.

As the darkness began to fade, all Julie knew was that her head hurt real bad. Had it hurt this much the first time she'd gotten electrocuted? That morning waking up in the strangest, most familiar room in the world seemed like an age ago now.

Indistinct shapes started to form in front of her. They seemed to be trying to talk to her, but their voices drifted in and out, like bad radio reception. Fuzzy.

Mmm, fuzzy, what a great word. Fuzzy. Julie started to drift away again.

"Julie! Stay with me." Shocked back into a world of pain, Julie opened her eyes again and this time the signal was loud and clear.

Crowded above her were the concerned faces of Johnnie, Iona, and Doug. She rolled her head to her right and saw Mr. Peterson clinging to Rosanna's lifeless body. Andrew leaned against the wall, shell-shocked.

Julie looked back to her Mom. "She's gone, isn't she?"

"I'm so sorry." As Iona gathered her up into the softest and warmest of hugs, Julie looked over her mom's shoulder at Rosanna's body. They'd never really thought they would stay, never thought that life would continue here when they were gone, never wondered what leaving would mean for the continuation of their lives here.

Or not.

Glancing up to heaven, she sent up a small, silent prayer for Rosanna's safe journey home.

* * *

Rosanna lay unconscious on the den carpet.

Early morning light drifted in through the blinds, over the debris of punctured beer cans, half-eaten carrot cake and vodka-smoothie dried hard onto the half a dozen or so glasses that rolled across the floor.

Next to Rosanna's prone form, the blackened Betamax VCR still faintly smoked and whirred.

CLUNK! The top-loading deck sprang open, waking Rosanna with a start.

She clapped a hand to her aching head, then started to push herself up from the floor, a trail of drool still connecting the side of her mouth to the carpet.

"Oh God." Feeling something very bad was about to happen, she forced herself upright on stiff legs and hobbled as fast as she could to the bathroom.

Washing her face after vomiting gave her a chance to check herself out in the mirror. Yup, every line, wrinkle, and crease was back, somehow seeming all the worse for having been on a week's vacation.

She twisted around, lifting herself up as high as she could to see in the small mirror... Yup, her old ass was back in place too.

What a spacey dream that was.

Rosanna stumbled back into the den and noticed for the first time that Julie was lying on the rug, out as cold as she had been a couple of minutes ago. She squatted down and gave Julie a gentle shake. "Hey Ju, wake up."

Geez, Rosanna's head was cracking. She drew a hand over her face and stuck her tongue out, trying to shake the sensation that something had crawled up and died in her mouth.

Then she noticed that Julie still wasn't moving. She shook her, with a little more urgency this time. "Julie, come on!"

With no response, she shook harder and harder, her voice rising with her panic. "Come on, Julie, no, come on!"

Before she even dialed 911, she could hear the sirens in her head, warning her too late of what it had meant when Julie chose to stay behind.

* * *

Julie's funeral was strange, beautiful and sad. To Rosanna it was almost like Julie really had died, because she was sure she'd never see her friend again. But she knew now that Julie was happy, in a different life.

And maybe that wasn't so different than death either – she just had a little more reassurance than your average believer.

Roger had wanted the plainest, most simple funeral, claiming that Julie 'wouldn't have wanted any fuss'. Trying to save himself the money, more like. Besides, trying not to make a fuss was what had gotten Julie into trouble her whole life.

So Rosanna ignored Roger's protests and filled the church with gorgeous, heavily scented flowers of all kinds and sizes, from hothouse orchids to wild things she'd found on the roadside and couldn't even name. Flowers that represented every side of Julie that she'd locked down and hidden away in this life: her wildness; her fecundity; her bright colors; her joy.

Rosanna hoped that, whatever life she was living now, Julie would never make herself small again.

Left alone now at the graveside, Rosanna turned from these thoughts to see Roger at the cemetery gates.

There was a vaguely familiar brunette by his side, pretty in a middle-aged, frowzy sort of way. Didn't she work at the Outlets with Roger?

Understanding dawned as she saw Roger's hand slowly, fake-casually, slide down the woman's back and settle tentatively on the rise of her ass. Before they'd even left the cemetery – Roger was all class, as ever.

Biting down the urge to run right over there and kick him where it wouldn't make any difference, Rosanna took a deep breath. Come on. *Zen*. At least this has released you from having to feel bad for that...that man.

She closed her eyes, breathed in deep and turned her whole self back to face Julie's grave. Opening her eyes again, she saw it covered with the wreaths and hanks of wild flowers laid there. One large daisy, in particular, seemed to wink at her in the sunshine, almost like it was laughing, throwing its head back in pure joy.

She looked up at the blue sky and gave up silent thanks.

* * *

And there's nothing like a funeral to kick-start a new beginning, Rosanna thought to herself as she looked into Gib's bedroom, trying not to sigh at the monumental task in front of her.

Everywhere she looked were dirty plates, tube socks, magazines (not the ones you hide under the bed – teenage boys don't need those these days, they have the internet...), ripped blu-ray discs that she really hoped were videogames and not more porn, candy bar wrappers, and strange mold experiments that probably used to be glasses of milk.

Could she do this? This went against the grain of everything she'd decided when she had Gib fifteen years ago – she was never going to be one of those moms that insisted on a tidy room, that went in that room, that invaded her kid's privacy.

But that was fifteen years ago and maybe it was time both her and Gib did a little growing up. So instead she thought about all the money missing from her pocket book, the grunts and cusses fired her way every time she attempted a conversation. All her attempts to be Gib's friend hadn't earned her any respect, so maybe it was time for a little parenting the old-fashioned way.

She picked up the plastic crate at her feet, unplugged Gib's beloved game console and tossed it in. There, that was number one.

Emboldened now, she moved through the room, picking up an iPod, a MacBook, any Blu-Ray discs that actually came in a case - even the occasional book, and shoved them all in.

* * *

When Gib got home, his mother had already hammered the 'yard sale' sign into the front lawn and was just carrying the last box out of the now-empty garage.

The lawn was covered in boxes and boxes of old clothes, redundant games consoles, CDs, books, a drum kit, wetsuits, three bodyboards and an aquarium complete with expensive oxygenation equipment.

Gib stopped to riffle through the nearest box and found his brand new MacBook looking back at him.

"Mom, what the hell are you doing?"

She smiled fondly back at him – obviously losing it. Old age, probably. Maybe she hit menopause already? Breaking off this thought, Gib realized she was still giving him that looper look and now she was talking at him.

"I'm having a yard sale so you can pay back all the money you owe me."

Gib looked at her blankly. What was the cray woman talking about?

And she was still talking.

"You know, the unauthorized loans from my wallet?"

Oh God! She was so uptight. Just cause he borrowed a couple of dollars. That money was important shit, like for fronting, out with the guys, what? And, whatever, because, like, "This is my stuff!"

There. Total slam-dunk argument.

But she was still smiling at him, all like blissed out and shit. Did she find his weed when she was clearing out all this stuff?

"Gib, honey, I love you, I really do."

Definitely smoked my weed, thought Gib. Or maybe

she took some X? Everybody was on X in the 90s, all of them, even his mom, probably. "But you don't deserve any of this stuff. You don't value it, you don't take care of any of it and you certainly haven't earned it."

What was she talking about now? "Who the hell's mom makes them earn it?"

"Well, yours, from now on. Yay!" She was nearly dancing a little dance there. "We're going to learn an important life lesson and become better people!"

Maybe she wasn't on drugs. Maybe she'd just OD-ed on *Glee* reruns. "This is bullshit."

He saw the smile waver. She was definitely wobbling. Soon have this in the bag.

"Well okay." *(See?* thought Gib, she's just about to cave.) "The best part is, you're going to have to get a Saturday job if you want to replace any of this stuff," (What?) "because I'm going part-time at work, so I'll have more time to paint in my new studio!"

She was pretty much hopping with excitement, or drugs, or whatever hormones the doctors give to old ladies to stop them drying up completely, and now she was pointing over her shoulder at this new 'studio', but all Gib could see was the empty garage.

"Want to help me decorate?"

"No!" Like, any more stupid questions?

"I'll pay you." Gib's interest picked up a bit. But only a little.

"You could earn some of this stuff back. I'll trade you the Xbox for five hours work. That's a whole lot better than minimum wage."

Seeing his favorite object in the whole world dangling in front of him, almost safe from his mother's nutty scheme, Gib considered. "It's second hand now - two hours."

"Well, you get points for quick thinking, so three and half hours and it's a deal."

Gib paused, seeing if he could stare her down to two and a half.

Nothing doing.

"Deal."

"Great!" She was off and moving again – maybe it was diet pills? He knew a few girls at school on those and they never stopped. "You can start by grabbing a couple of those packs of TSP over there and fill a bucket with water – hot water – and soap down the walls and ceiling."

Sighing loudly, so his mom would totally get the point, Gib slouched off to get the hot water.

One day, when he was rich and famous, he would totally tell this story all over the internet and everyone would know what a nut his mom was and they'd all want his story about how he'd succeeded against the odds and been really nice to his crazy mom who thought her garage was a 'studio' for 'art'.

Yeah, this would totally make people see how, like, he survived some really tough shit and he was still a great guy. And sensitive. Yeah, girls love sensitive.

* * *

Suppressing a sigh of her own, Rosanna turned back to the boxes and got down on her hunkers to sort through them.

It wasn't all Gib's stuff. Rummaging through a stack of DVDs, she found a copy of *Pretty in Pink* and her smile widened to a grin.

As she read through the familiar blurb on the back on the case ('And Duckie's Pretty Crazy!'), a shadow fell across the box. "Got any good movies in there?"

Looking up to see who was asking, she squinted up at the man silhouetted against the sun. As her eyes adjusted, he started to look familiar. He started to look like… But it couldn't be. It wasn't.

But it was.

22

Falling back on her ass in shock, Rosanna blinked up at Andrew. An older, more weathered Andrew, but most definitely Andrew. Here. On her front lawn. In reality.

Huh.

She searched for the right words. "Andrew? What the hell?"

He looked down at her, smiling like he just couldn't stop. "I ran into Julie's little brother, Phil, a couple of weeks ago."

Phil? Rosanna racked her brain. "Do you mean Scooter?"

"Oh, yeah, no I don't think he likes anyone to call him that now he's working for NASA. Pretty serious stuff, all top secret, apparently."

He seemed to drift off, looking at Rosanna as if he was trying to find some sort of clue in her face. Maybe just checking out the crow's feet. Rosanna couldn't hold back, "And?"

He seemed to snap out of his reverie. "Oh, yeah, and he told me how I could find you. And here you are."

Suddenly he seemed to realize that she was still sitting on her ass on the lawn.

He reached out a hand to her and pulled her up so that all at once she was right up close to him, chest to chest, almost nose to nose. His body was more solid than she remembered. His smell was different too – not so much cheap aftershave and sweat, more wood smoke and amber.

"You grew up."

Andrew laughed. "I kinda needed to."

"Well, yeah."

He leaned in to kiss her and she felt her body pull towards him, but she held back a moment and looked him in the eye. "Weren't you surprised? I mean, didn't you think I was, you know—?"

"Dead?" She saw a shadow cross his face. "Yeah, I did think that. In fact, I pretty clearly remember going to your funeral." He smiled, but he didn't look amused. "Like I said, Phil's work, it's all hush-hush stuff. I had to sign a lot of paperwork and if I told you, I'd probably have to kill you."

"Except I'm already dead."

He smiled again, and this time it was genuine. "Well, nobody's perfect."

"I heard someone say that, yeah." Rosanna finally allowed herself to relax into his arms and moved closer to take that sweet, warm kiss.

It was definitely worth the wait.

Epilogue

Even so, there was still one more thing Rosanna needed to know.

Just back from the store, she slipped the brand new Blu-Ray case out of its plastic wrap, took out the disc and slid it into the player.

Kicking back on the couch, Andrew spotted the smoke-blackened Betamax player under the TV. "What happened to that? It looks kind of fried."

Rosanna turned around from fiddling with the Blu-Ray. "We are not touching that. Ever again. But I just have to watch the end of this movie, it's really important."

She turned and gave him the big puppy dog eyes. "Please?"

"You don't want to watch the whole thing?"

Rosanna smiled an inward smile. "I don't really need to."

Sitting down and snuggling tight into the crook of Andrew's arm, Rosanna pointed the remote and started to navigate the menus till she found what she needed to see.

JULIE – WHAT HAPPENED NEXT

As Julie reached as high as she could with the paint roller duct-taped to the end of her broom handle, familiar hands reached around her, sliding inside her denim overalls and caressing the swelling bump where her baby moved and stretched to the touch.

Surprised but pleased, she turned to kiss Johnnie, missing his lips and catching the tip of his nose.

"Hey," he chided gently, "I thought we agreed you weren't doing any more painting till after Mr. Potato makes an appearance."

"No, we agreed I wouldn't climb any more ladders."

Julie turned in the circle of his arms to kiss him properly. "And if you think any painting is gonna get done after Mr. – or Miss – Potato is here, you gotta be kidding."

Julie loved the tiny apartment she and Johnnie had moved into after their town hall wedding.

Sure, you could cross it in a couple of steps, and it was above a laundromat in Chinatown – the Hilton it certainly was not – but she'd been happier here than she could have imagined in any showhome or mansion you could offer.

That said, the place had needed a lot of work.

But after the dirty, torn lino had all been ripped out, the evidence of years of heavy smoking tenants scrubbed from the walls and ceilings, the window frames sanded and freshly painted, all she had to do was put a good coat of paint on the walls.

Then she had plans for the corner of the bedroom that was the baby's; a delicate mural of toy trains and teddy bears painted around a dilapidated crib that she'd found in a thrift shop and painstakingly restored.

She sighed with satisfaction as she contemplated the home she was making for her, Johnnie and the new life that was slowly growing inside her.

God, if only they offered gender scans in the 1980s –

she could hardly wait to find out if it was a boy or a girl! Still, only a couple of weeks to go...

The only fly in her ointment was that her mom and dad were not happy.

Well, in Doug's case, that was definitely an understatement. Iona was determined to make the best of everything, but Doug's fury simmered barely below the surface, erupting at regular intervals. It didn't help to point out that Doug and Iona themselves had made exactly the same mistakes...

Johnnie saw the shadow cross her face.

He turned her around again until she could see herself in the full-length mirror stood in the corner of the room, to reflect some light onto Julie's handiwork. "Look at you. At both of you. Have you ever seen anything so beautiful?"

Julie blushed, looking away. "Hardly – look at me, I'm enormous! My butt could get its own zip code."

Johnnie stifled a laugh, knowing better (by now) than to mock Julie when she was feeling vulnerable and hormonal. "Now, you know that's not true. You look exactly the same as you always did, just with a little more luggage up front."

She smiled wryly, knowing that really it was true. Didn't stop her feeling like a circus freak, though. "I'll just be glad when I can wear shoes that lace up again. And I don't need a stool in the shower like a little old lady!"

Her reverie on the discomforts of late pregnancy was broken by a buzz on the intercom. Then she remembered – Oh shit! Her parents were coming to visit! It was the first time Doug had agreed to come to the apartment since the wedding.

Before she had time to so much as straighten the curtains, Johnnie was opening the door and in they came, Iona leading the way. She had already decided that she would find the good in everything she saw; Doug hung back, determined to find fault.

"Is this the whole of it?" She saw her mom dig him in the ribs.

Julie whipped the dustsheets off the couch and started to dismantle the paint roller/broom handle rig. "Well, I was just about to make us some coffee. Would anyone like coffee?"

Realizing she was in serious danger of babbling, she clamped her mouth shut and ran the three steps to the kitchenette to put the pot on the stove.

Behind her, she could hear her father talking to Johnnie, "So, I hear you're doing a good job with the computer inventory. The fellas at the mill say you know your stuff." Julie smiled to herself. – Doug was obviously under strict instructions to make an effort this time.

Julie laid up a big tray with coffee, cream and sugar cookies and got two steps back before Johnnie rushed to take the heavy load from her. "Hey, you're making me look bad here."

He kissed her cheek as he took the tray and, over his shoulder Julie could see her mother smile warmly even as her father rolled his eyes.

Iona clasped Johnnie's hand as he set down the tray beside her. "So, I hear you're taking night classes at the adult ed. center on Michigan?"

"That's right, ma'am." Johnnie smiled nervously, anxious to make a better impression with Julie's parents than he seemed to have so far. "Computer programming, every Monday, Wednesday and Friday night. I could still have my college degree in four years' time."

"And what's Julie doing while you're out making your dreams come true?" Suddenly even the thinnest facade of good humor dropped from Doug's face. "There any space in this cozy set up for what Julie wants?"

"Dad!" How to explain? "This is exactly what I want. It's what I've always wanted."

"This?" Doug's voice was low, but his color rose dangerously high. "Well, I always knew that Ginny only ever wanted to chase after boys and get married, but you? I thought you were more like your mother; thought you'd want something more out of life."

Julie could feel her temper rising. She sprang up, toe to toe with her father now. "Well, it's not over yet! You're just mad I'm making the same mistakes you did!"

"Of course I am!" Doug was really shouting now. "Why would I want him to mess up your life like I messed up your mother's—"

"Doug!" Iona's hand flew to her mouth. But Doug wasn't listening. He was looking down curiously at the water that had just splashed all over his dark brown suede shoes. He looked up again.

"Julie?"

* * *

Outside the delivery suite, Doug and Iona sat quietly on uncomfortable plastic chairs and drank little cups of coffee from the hospital vending machine, not even noticing the foul taste or the tongue blistering heat.

From the mad dash to the hospital in Doug's car, to getting Julie into delivery and then supporting her through the first stages of labor, they had barely paused for breath.

But Julie's epidural had just kicked in and after ten hours of labor, she was taking the chance for a nap before the real hard work began.

Sliding her hand gently into Doug's, Iona was the first to break the silence.

"Is that what you really thought all this time?"

"What?" Dazed by the previous ten hours and by seeing his little girl in so much pain, Doug had no idea what Iona could mean.

"What you said at Julie's apartment. That you ruined my life?" She rested her head on his shoulder, apprehensive of his reply.

"Well, didn't I?"

Doug turned and, putting his fingers gently under her chin, tipped her head so that her eyes couldn't but meet his. "You were going to write songs, play guitar, tour the world in that crappy old bus of your cousin Artie's. Then I came along, and you got stuck here your whole life."

"Stuck here?" Iona's eyes pricked with tears. "Don't you know anything? You idiot" She sighed. "I love it here. I love our kids; I love our life. I even love you when you're not being such an ass."

Swinging her foot to the side, she gently kicked him on the ankle.

Doug sat in silence, Iona's words sinking in. She

turned and looked up at his bewildered face. "Besides, like Julie said, it's not over yet. I'm only thirty-eight years old."

Doug kissed her forehead. "Still look nineteen to me." He mulled it over. "So, you still want to go on the road in Artie's van?"

"No!" Iona's whole body creased in laughter at the thought of Artie's beat-up old rust bucket – if it was even still in one piece. "But I still got stuff I want to do. If those two kids in there can work it out," she nodded towards the delivery room, "I'm sure we can too."

As she spoke, the doors to the delivery suite burst open, and Johnnie's face appeared, wild-eyed and even wilder of hair. "It's time. Mrs. Placid, she wants you."

* * *

Much later, as Julie lay sleeping against a mountain of soft, white pillows, Johnnie stared in awe at the tiny creature in his arms. Slatey eyes squinted suspiciously up at him from a tiny, scrunched, red face.

A miracle.

He looked up at a gentle knock on the door, and Iona poked her head around. "There's someone else here would like to see the baby – can we come in?"

Opening the door wider, she revealed Mr. Peterson, looking strangely shy as he clutched a bundle of pink balloons. "Your mom, ah, your mother-in-law told me, so I went back to the gift shop."

He hesitated. "I expect you've got a load already, I'll take these back, it's silly."

"No, no, no!" Johnnie rushed forward to take Mr. Peterson's arm and steered him into the room. His voice dropped to a whisper. "Julie will love these, she's just taking a little nap after...you know. She's pretty tired."

"It's okay, I'm awake already." Julie opened one eye, then saw Mr. Peterson and sat up with a warm smile. She hadn't seen much of him since the funeral, but she tried to keep an eye on him, for Rosanna's sake. "Come in, we've got someone wants to meet you."

She took the baby girl from Johnnie and very gently laid her in Mr. Peterson's arms. He looked terrified. "It's been a long time since I did this."

Looking down into the eyes of the baby girl, he didn't notice various meaningful eyebrow raises and gestures pass between Johnnie and Julie, until Johnnie cleared his throat. "Ah, Mr. Peterson, we've got something we want to tell you—"

"Well, ask you, really," Julie broke in. "We'd like to - if it's alright with you - we'd like to call her Rosanna."

For a moment, Mr. Peterson was so silent, so still, Julie was afraid.

When he finally looked up, there were tears in his eyes. Oh no, thought Julie, too much. We messed this up.

Then he broke into a tearful smile that lit up his whole face from within. "That's alright with me." He turned back to look at baby Rosanna again, wriggling in his arms. "That's alright with me."

* * *

As Rosanna watched Julie and her family leave the hospital, pile into Doug's station wagon and drive into the sunset (and the credits started to roll) her heart was heavy with love and loss.

This really was the last glimpse she'd get of her

friend, which she'd guess was more than most people got when the person they loved was gone, so the sadness of loss was mingled with joy, with hope and a new trust that the future would find its own strange way of working itself out.

She turned to Andrew. There was just one thing that was still bugging her.

"You never did tell me. Why did you get kicked out of high school?"

"Well…"

THE END

Acknowledgements

My thanks to all the people who have read and provided valuable feedback on the various versions of this story over the last three years including: Rachel 'Mimey Vice' Evans and Lucy 'Roisin Roulette' Harkness-Taylor of my beloved Birmingham Blitz Dames roller derby league; all the members of the West Oxfordshire Writers Group; the Oxford Screenwriters' Group; Trevor Butterworth and, of course, my husband, Karl Schweppe.

Thanks to Claire 'Blake' White of BlakeDesigns.co.uk for helping me out with promotional materials.

Valuable professional feedback was also received on early drafts from Danny Manus at No Bullscript Consulting.

Spot-on Cover Design by Alexander John

The Films that Inspired the Book

I'm sure many of those who've read this far will already have spotted the references and asides to many, many classic 80s teen movies that pepper Julie and Rosanna's story.

But just in case you're dying to confirm your guesses, or just want to revisit those films again, here is a full list of the films that directly influenced the text:

- *Pretty in Pink* (Howard Deutch, 1986). Of course, for without Duckie, there would be no Johnnie.

- *Sixteen Candles* (John Hughes, 1984). John Hughes' first outing with Molly Ringwald – watch it again to see which background characters and throwaway jokes inspired me.

- *The Sure Thing* (Rob Reiner, 1985). A classic John Cusack RomCom and, in my opinion, better than *Say Anything* (she says as she ducks for cover to avoid flying fruit…)

- *The Terminator* (James Cameron, 1984). Okay, not strictly speaking a teen movie but what would the eighties have been without The Terminator? I couldn't resist…

- *Weird Science* (John Hughes, 1985). A film that is so wrong, on so many levels, but I can't resist watching it again every time it's on the box. Many years later I was still trying to convince my sister that I really did see a movie where the guy's brother was turned into a giant talking turd…

- *Ferris Bueller's Day Off* (John Hughes, 1986). The titan of 80s teen movies. And writing this list really makes you realise, John Hughes had a very busy decade.
- *Fast Times at Ridgemont High* (Amy Heckerling, 1982). So many classic moments, and so many scenes that wouldn't make it into a teen movie today.
- *Heathers* (Michael Lehmann, 1988). Blink and you'll miss the paté reference, but well done if you spotted it – you win my undying nerd kudos.
- *Better Off Dead* (Savage Steve Holland, 1985). Glossing over the heavy metal hamburger scene...
- *Say Anything* (Cameron Crowe, 1989). It always helps to have someone in mind when you're writing a character and – given the choice – I would always have cast John Mahoney as Mr. Peterson.
- *Gremlins* (Joe Dante, 1984). Again, if you spot this reference, my endless admiration goes to you.

Of course, there were a lot of other 80s movies that I watched while writing this story in the interests of (ahem) research, but not every joke or aside fitted with the story so a lot of cutting went on.

If you'd like to find out more about the influences behind this book, why there was more swearing in 1980s teen movies and how to dry freeze a koosh ball, check out my blog – Trappedinan80steenmovie.com – or follow me on Twitter - @Trapped80sMovie.

Copyright Notices

Copyright © 2014 Michelle Duffy
All Rights Reserved

Printed in Germany
by Amazon Distribution
GmbH, Leipzig